SUPER NORMAL

Josh Denslow

STILL
HOUSE
PRESS

All inquiries may be directed to:

> Stillhouse Press
> 4400 University Drive, 3E4
> Fairfax, VA 22030
> www.stillhousepress.org

Stillhouse Press is an independent, student- and alumni-run nonprofit press based out of Northern Virginia and operated in collaboration with Watershed Lit: Center for Literary Engagement and Publishing Practice at George Mason University.

Library of Congress Control Number: 2023935424

ISBN-13:   978-1-945233-0-3 Paperback
             978-1-945233-21-0 eBook

Cover Design: Megan Lynn Brooks and Linda Hall
Cover Art:
    Sketch of bee © BigJoy/Adobe Stock
    Full color bee © olegganko/ Adobe Stock
    Cape © designer_things / Adobe stock
    Honey comb © JC/ Adobe Stock
Interior Layout: Carol Mitchell

This final, final, final version of the novel is for Rebecca.
And now she never has to read it again.

ADVANCE PRAISE FOR *SUPER NORMAL*

Whether they are linked by blood or circumstance, each of the absorbing, effortlessly charming characters in *Super Normal* share the same exuberant, inexhaustible desire for connection. Denslow's prose is empathetic and endlessly witty—this novel deftly explores grief, longing, and the actual magic of one unforgettable family.

    - Kimberly King Parsons, author of *Black Light*

Josh Denslow has done something remarkable here. *Super Normal* is a beautiful debut novel about what it takes to love and accept ourselves and each other, written with real care and big-heartedness and attention to what makes us human.

    - Matthew Salesses, author of *The Sense of Wonder*

Josh Denslow does something brilliant in *Super Normal,* using the magic of superheroes not to render the world in some new and fantastical way, but to allow us to see how mysterious and beautiful and sometimes heartbreaking the bonds of family are, what we inherit, who we hold onto, how we keep running away from and back to the people who made us. With such a sharp wit and a sense of when to allow that humor to transform to address the heaviness of the story, Denslow has constructed a wonderful novel that you can't put down.

    - Kevin Wilson, author of *Nothing to See Here*

Denslow has not only masterfully layered multiple narratives to gradually converge into this epic super-moment, he's also captured the snappy dialogue and sharp humor that make comics and graphic novels so delightful to read. Denslow has accomplished a dynamic, heart-warming book about grief and family that will rekindle your faith in humanity. This is a super-memorable, super-entertaining, super-novel that is, despite its title, anything but super-normal."

    - Kalani Pickhart, author of *I Will Die in a Foreign Land*

Josh Denslow has written a novel that is one third superhero story, one third contemporary bildungsroman, and one third prickly rose bush. The characters alternate between scratching and drawing blood and budding and blossoming in each other's presence in a way that will be hard for readers to put down.

    - Megan Giddings, author of *The Women Could Fly*

Day One

THE HEROES ASSEMBLE

CHAPTER ONE

CATAPULTING INTO THE PAST

1

Beth was free.

Unfortunately, freedom meant picking up McDonald's french fries on the way out of town and then feeling so guilty about buying them that she'd let them grow cold in the passenger seat. The salt and grease sparkled in the light from her phone which had vibrated every minute after she first left, and then after a couple of hours of driving, had vibrated every ten, then every twenty minutes. There was no way Beth was answering, and there was no way she was turning it off. She wanted to be wanted and missed and chased as the smell of the french fries permeated every porous surface in the car and her entire face.

At first, she hadn't known where she was going. She drove on and off the highway at random, like those little lottery balls in the air machines which never spit out the numbers that matched Beth's ticket. But after the McDonald's stop and the first fifty missed calls from Fran, Beth admitted she'd known where she was going but hadn't built up the courage to go there yet.

Then, like magic, she was home.

The house was completely dark as Beth got out of the car holding her phone in one hand and the cold fries in the other. The house had never been anything special, one of hundreds of houses that looked nearly identical. Years ago, when the neighborhood was first assembled, some families opted for the covered front porch, some the two-car garage, some the large upstairs window in the master bedroom, and they all chose between four vaguely different hues of blue for the siding. No house stood out. And none of them contained a family like Beth's.

At the moment, Beth's family home looked as if no one had been there in weeks. And like anyone who had fled home while screaming at her mother and throwing everything that tied her to her family in a pile by the door, Beth didn't have a key.

She knocked. She rang the bell. The house remained silent and dark and uninviting. As if her past didn't want her.

But being unwanted had never stopped Beth before. She tried the door handle. Locked. She stepped onto the little porch and tried opening the window that her brother Taylor had broken twice when they were kids, only to discover it was locked as well. She walked past the garage and around to the chain link fence her mom had erected after their dad had died.

In the dark, the backyard looked slightly overgrown. No one used a weed whacker along the fence anymore. The umbrella inserted into the table on the porch had broken at some point and jutted out like the front of a train. She tried the back sliding glass door. It was locked too.

Beth returned to the driveway and looked at her phone. It had been a half hour since Fran's last call. One text: Come back.

She scrolled through her directory and found her sister Denise's number.

"I almost didn't answer," Denise said. "But curiosity killed a cat, and I hate cats."

"I'm sorry it's been so long," Beth said, her back to the house now. She surveyed the neighborhood in which she'd ridden her bike and fought Claire Perkins and walked her dog that had gotten hit by a car. It was becoming a little overwhelming.

"Are you in AA or something?" Denise said. "Is this one of those calls?"

"No. But kind of you to think I'd need outside stimulus to call and say hello."

"Oh, you're just saying hello? Cool. No need to discuss your complete disappearance at all. Well then. Hello right back to you."

Then before Beth could acknowledge what was happening, she was crying. Not loud or anything. Just some tears and a thickness in her throat. But Denise knew. She definitely knew.

"Where are you?" Denise asked.

"I'm home, Denise. I'm home. But no one's home and I can't get in."

"It's parent-teacher conferences at school. Mom won't be there for an hour or so," Denise said.

Beth hated the neediness clutching her heart. "What about you? Can you swing by?"

"I'm here too. At the school."

Beth felt a rush of sadness. How had she missed Denise having a child? "Boy or girl?" she asked.

"Really funny," Denise said. "Wait, did you think I'd somehow squeezed out a kid since we last spoke?"

"I guess not," Beth said. "Well, I'm out front then. Locked out. Holding cold french fries."

"Does Mom know you're coming?" Denise asked.

"No. And please don't tell her. I guess it will be a surprise."

"Mom hates surprises."

Beth wiped the last of the tears from her eyes. "Let me catch her off guard then. She doesn't need to be preparing a speech for me."

Denise chuckled. "I hear you. Okay. You planning to stick around? Will I see you?"

"You'll see me."

After they hung up, Beth stared at her phone. The screen was as dark as her childhood home. Beth thought it would take much longer than this for Fran to give up. At least a year. Or six months. But it had been a few hours and already her phone was totally silent.

Beth walked to the other side of the driveway and looked up at her bedroom window. She wondered what her mom had done with all of her stuff. The movie posters and VHS tapes and CDs. Would she have kept them in a box in the basement or would she have dropped them at Goodwill?

A car drove by and illuminated the front of the house. Beth looked at her mom's window upstairs and saw that it was halfway open.

She put her phone in her pocket, placed the fries gently in the grass, and bent her knees slightly. She bobbed up and down a little. She knew she could still do it. It wasn't something a person forgets. She shook her hands out to her sides. She closed her eyes and took a deep breath.

Then she launched herself into the air.

It took a moment to reacquaint herself with the balance needed to fly. It had been years since she'd done more than drift a little off the scale to cut a few pounds or boost herself up to a higher shelf in the kitchen. Now here she was, gliding in the evening air, and it felt like all the shackles holding her to the earth had been severed. She was flying above all of it. She never had to design another brochure for the university again. She didn't have to create style guidelines for every single goddamn department. She would never again be asked for the hex codes for the school colors. And if Fran wanted to celebrate her promotion without her, then Beth would show her what it was like to not be together at all.

A car whipped around the corner, and Beth lurched toward the open window; that old fear of being caught sweeping through her, the same fear she had felt when her mom had walked into her room while Beth had her hand fully down Claire Perkins's jeans.

Beth steadied herself and pushed the screen into her mom's room where it slapped against the flowery comforter on her mom's bed. She managed to insert her body after it before the car's headlights could give her away.

Beth lay on the floor, the smell of her mom's floral perfume clinging to every particle of air, as if bear hugging them into submission.

The tears returned but she wasn't sure if she was laughing or crying now.

2

Denise sat at a metal teacher's desk in a half-darkened room at her mom's elementary school. The chalkboard behind her was perfectly clean; not a hint of chalk dust anywhere. Denise could pull up a whole sensory checklist of how it felt to stay after class and bang erasers together, the chalk sprinkling her hair and coating her throat, and then dunking a moth-eaten rag into a bucket filled with lukewarm water and swiping it across the chalkboard, the green color darkening the wetter it got. But when she was done, she'd step back and admire her work. Even though she'd been in trouble, detained after class for talking back or pushing someone around, there was a sense of pride that Denise could tap into now, years later. A sense of accomplishment that swelled her chest and flushed her cheeks. She had conquered the chalkboard. The chalkboard was her bitch.

There wasn't much in her life that she conquered these days. Most noticeably, her finances. Sure, it was embarrassing, but Denise had come to rely on the monthly checks from her mom. Almost as if just existing as her daughter was a part-time job. But last month no check had come and another month was about to pass. Denise had shown up at parent-teacher night with the thought of confronting her mom, or at least asking nicely if she could keep the money flowing.

The door to the room banged open, startling Denise enough for her to slam her knee into the underside of the metal desk.

"Oh God," the man in the doorway said. "Are you okay?" He was tall with hunched shoulders, as if he were permanently trying to lean down to everyone else's level. But his face had a handsome fragility, almost feminine, with an endearing grin even while he was expressing concern. Despite her throbbing knee, Denise wanted to know if he wore boxers or briefs.

"Just whacked my knee," she said. "Good thing all the blood is rushing to my head in embarrassment. That should take care of any pain."

They stared awkwardly at each other. Neither knew if they were supposed to keep talking to each other or part ways.

"I'm John," he said.

"How did you get parent-teacher duty tonight?" Denise said. "Did your bowling league go late last week or something?"

"I have all the duties. I'm a single dad."

"Oh, the quick reveal," Denise said.

"You didn't tell me your name."

"Denise."

John nodded as if her name confirmed something he'd been thinking. "How did you get parent-teacher duty then? Your book club run late last week? Or something."

Denise scoffed. "Come on. I don't have a kid. My mom is Mrs. Clark. I'm here to heckle her during the meetings. I'll yell out: Mrs. Clark doesn't know her multiplication tables. Or: Mrs. Clark reads at a third-grade level."

John laughed. "I'll see you in there then. She's my son's teacher. But I didn't know those things about her."

"She hides it well."

Another silence rushed over them. Denise wondered if it might go on forever. As if they'd been vacuum sealed together.

"I don't really talk to very many people," John said.

"You don't have to play the sympathy card," Denise said. "I'll get a drink with you."

John's face flushed red. "Really? When?"

"Tonight. After this madness."

This John guy seemed nice, but it was more than that. Denise knew Beth was sitting out in front of their childhood home, apparently crying, and waiting for Denise to rescue her. Their mom was going to implode or explode or at least go apoplectic with rage when she saw Beth, and now here was this unassuming guy to distract Denise from all of that.

"I'll have to tell the babysitter," John said.

"Just give her a lot of money when you get home late."

John's arms waved around and his mouth opened and closed a couple of times. Clearly he didn't know what to say after successfully setting up a date.

"I'll meet you in the parking lot after this wraps up," Denise said.

"I'm looking forward to it," John said.

"Don't be earnest and ruin everything," Denise said.

"Will do." Then he turned and banged the door closed behind him.

Securing a date was not the intended outcome of the evening. Now she had to figure out how to pay if he called her bluff when she offered to pay her half. She got up from the metal desk, her knee throbbing slightly, and looked out the fingerprint-covered window. Three women were smoking on the swings, their purses forgotten on a bench behind them. Should be easy enough.

Denise slipped into the hallway and her shoes squeaked on the tiles as she made her way to the dented metal door. Just before stepping outside, she tightened what she thought of as an extra muscle, and with a little applied pressure, Denise disappeared.

She could still see herself, which had caused some confusion when she was younger and had been trying to spy on her friends or sneak out of the house. Beth was the one who had actually come up with the idea of thinking of her power as a muscle. Flex it and Denise became invisible. Anything she was wearing or holding came along with her, so if anyone happened to be looking where she was standing next to the basketball hoop, they would see no one. Not even a shadow.

The three women were still smoking and laughing and twisting on their swings. Their purses were like seed pods waiting to be opened.

Denise walked quietly to the bench and reached into the first one, hoping that the wallet was on top and she didn't have to dig around too much for it. And she hoped it was full of cash.

3

Edna loved the kids in her sixth grade class with a fierceness that sometimes surprised her. She snapped at a fellow teacher who had the audacity to claim that one of her students was obstinate. She noticed one of her students wasn't eating lunch and she began secretly sliding money into her backpack each morning. She'd given more than one student new shoes when theirs were so worn the soles were coming apart. And she'd tutored and lectured and cajoled for hundreds of accumulated hours after class to make sure no one was ever left behind in their lessons.

That was why all of their parents, every last one over the decades Edna had been teaching, was an utter disappointment. All of her kids deserved better. They deserved parents who saw their potential. Who lit a fire under their creativity. Who pushed them to achieve more than they ever could imagine. Instead, they got parents who worked full-time and yawned during parent-teacher conferences or disagreed with Edna's assessment, as if she didn't know their children better than they ever would.

And so, as one parent after another revealed how little they understood their children, it was almost a relief to see Denise skulking around the proceedings but never approaching. Edna could take a moment between meetings to reflect on what a disappointment she was to her own daughter, in fact, to all three of her children, and how no matter how hard parents tried, they spent their lives letting their children down.

She looked up from her reverie. Which parent was she talking to?

"Are you okay, Mrs. Clark?" Phillip's dad said. "You look kind of ashen. Or, I don't know, maybe nauseated. Can I get you a bottle of water or something?"

"I'm getting old and losing color. I'll be in black and white soon," Edna said and swallowed a glob of bile that had been working its way up her throat.

Phillip's dad smiled, but he looked concerned. He had something in there, a sparkle in his sad eyes. Potential for greatness. He would have been a great student when he was younger, but life appeared to have been rough on him.

"Are you sure?" He squinted at her.

"Yes, thank you. You're a kind man. That's where Phillip gets it from."

Phillip's dad nodded. "So he's doing okay?"

"He's lovely. One of my favorites." That just slipped out. Edna wasn't supposed to say things like that. But of all her students, Phillip was the one she wanted to protect most. He reminded her of her own son, Taylor, who she hadn't seen in years. The bile covered a lump of sadness in her stomach. She really was coming apart.

"That's so great to hear. I just want him to succeed."

Edna felt a warmth spread through her. She reached out and took his hand. Also not technically allowed, but there was no going back now. "He will," she said. "He absolutely will."

Phillip's dad looked exhausted. She wanted to hug him. It had been so long since she'd had any physical contact with anyone. God, she was fucking lonely.

Edna expected Denise to accost her at her car, but she had left. If Edna wasn't mistaken, she'd gone off with Phillip's dad, which maybe wasn't the worst idea for her. He needed saving, and Denise needed to save someone. But one thing Denise definitely did not need was checks from Edna anymore. That was surely why Denise had come tonight. To ask why the fountain had stopped.

The problem was, Edna couldn't really answer that question herself. She felt different. It actually wasn't that she was coming apart, it was that she was coming together. Her past was accreting in any available space it could find inside her. Everything reminded her of past slights and grievances, and the anger was threatening to explode from every pore. Her head throbbed with it. Her fingers ached. Her back twisted. She was angry at Denise for needing her so much. For never figuring out life. Edna was ashamed of her own complicity. She made Denise who she was, just as she had made Beth and Taylor. When her husband Nolan had died, he'd taken with him a magical WD40 that had made her connections to her children less abrasive and squeaky. But with her mind now unfettered, every single decision she'd ever made could spark self-loathing. Edna was boiling alive.

Edna's car rattled across town while she tried some breathing techniques she'd learned on the Internet. But she knew the only thing that could calm her down. It was the little file of videos on her desktop. The ones from the adult site. The ones where humanity was aligned with the animal world. The ones that made her forget everything.

A few months ago, Edna discovered via the Internet that the only position she and Nolan had ever tried was Missionary. His sinewy body on top of her, his sweat beading on his brow and dripping into her tangled hair. Edna spent her evenings in floral nightgowns researching sexual positions on various websites. She enjoyed the way pornography flushed her cheeks and turned her heart into a beacon. It was nice to discover how alive she still was on the inside.

She could do without all the bodily fluids, the seemingly never-ending cavalcade of videos supplied. She'd like to see more of their faces. The reckless enjoyment. Sometimes she'd crank the speakers as high as her little computer would go so she could feel the moaning. She and Nolan had never said a word during intercourse.

What would Nolan have thought of online pornography? He surely wouldn't have approved. After he'd died, Edna had not discovered a secret stash of magazines. No letters from secret women. No hate-filled propaganda books. She'd spent weeks going through his things. Cataloging them. She'd wanted to find something that would give her permission to hate him as much as she already did for leaving her alone.

Alone with their children.

When Edna pulled into the garage, she could feel the pull of that secret folder on her computer. Her nerves buzzed and jangled. Anticipation blocking out the night and causing her to overlook the small carton of french fries in the grass. She grabbed her purse and opened the door into the house.

There was Beth.

The sudden appearance of an unexpected human in her house caused a full throb of shock to radiate throughout her body. Then, riding a wave of adrenaline, Edna brushed past her and shakily placed her purse on the dining table.

"How did you get in?" Edna said.

"Nice to see you, too, Mom," Beth said.

"Apologies are nicer than sarcasm."

Beth pressed her palms over her eyes, just like when she was a little girl, and sighed. "Of course. I will give you an apology. I will own it. But I hope you might consider giving me one too."

"You blame me for your dad's death and then renounce your status in our family. You throw all your shit in a pile on the porch and storm off like a little girl who was told she can't watch her favorite show. If I have anything to apologize for, it would be that I didn't make my house harder to break into."

Beth was stunned into silence. Edna almost felt bad, but she couldn't find her equilibrium.

"I can't do this tonight," Edna said. "Just stay. I know that's all you want. Just stay. Your room is exactly the same. I hope I can't say the same thing about you."

After a regretful glance at her computer in the front room, Edna went upstairs to submerge herself in her anger while pondering how being cast in the role of mother caused her to allow Beth to stay when no part of her actually wanted anyone there.

CHAPTER TWO

SATIATING THE MUNCH MONSTER

1

Just as her mother had said, Beth's bedroom was exactly as she'd left it over ten years earlier. Movie posters covered the walls and anime DVDs filled the bookshelf and clothes were heaped on the floor of the closet and Beth wasn't sure if she should feel honored or forgotten.

Her mom certainly hadn't forgotten her anger. Over the years it had come to a thick, soupy boil. But the reunion had gone better than Beth expected. She had figured they'd argue until a newspaper thwacked onto the driveway in the diffuse light of morning. She also figured she'd end up sleeping in her car. So Beth was technically winning.

Alone in her bedroom, a creepily perfect time capsule of a previous life, Beth was unmoored and doubting everything. It was as if she'd gone through a tesseract or that she'd successfully achieved 121 gigawatts of power and had been blasted into the past. She'd left Fran and her job and anything she couldn't fit in the car, and time traveled to the exact moment she'd previously done the same thing. A movie montage of her most spectacular failures. She remembered, back then, pulling over at the end of their street and aching to go back. To apologize to her mom. Now she felt the same ache, and she wanted to drive back to Fran. To apologize. But Beth didn't double back. Ever.

She wished she hadn't left the fries outside.

Beth picked up her phone. There was no one she could talk to. No one she hadn't cast aside. Well, almost no one.

Denise picked up on the fifth ring.

"Yet again I didn't want to answer but I had to know. How did it go with Mom?"

"Terrible. She hates me," Beth said. "But I'm in my old room."

"Creepy, right?" Denise said, her voice hushed.

"Exactly how I described it," Beth said.

"If you check in the hallway closet, under some towels on the top shelf, I have a bottle of tequila hidden there. Not much left."

"That's the nicest thing anyone has ever said to me." Beth felt it again. The tears. It was so annoying.

"You know I would have been there for you, right? After you left. That was between you and Mom. I would have been there for you. I looked up to you."

It was agony trying to hold in the tears. "I know."

Beth listened to the sound of Denise's breath. The ruffle of sheets. She was in bed and she had picked up anyway.

"I've been having nightmares," Beth said.

"About what?"

"Hotdogs."

"Hotdogs?"

"Among other talking foods. Last night there was a Pop-Tart."

"God, I love Pop-Tarts. Was it frosted?"

"They make them without frosting?" Beth said.

"Some people are monsters," Denise said.

"The Pop-Tart said, 'It would be an honor to be partially masticated by you and then dissolved by your stomach acids.'"

"An honor?" Denise said.

"How about 'partially masticated'? As if I don't chew my food properly."

"You're upset at a dream Pop-Tart for slighting your chewing skills?"

Beth thought for a moment. "Yes. I am."

"You really haven't changed."

Which was the furthest thing from what Beth wanted to hear.

2

After the call with Beth, Denise rolled over and found John sleeping with his mouth open like the final hole at mini-golf. He was there, of course, because it was his bed. Whenever Denise wanted to know if someone wore boxers or briefs, she always found out.

This time it was boxers.

John hadn't believed her when she'd said she'd come to his house after his son Phillip had gone to bed. But that's exactly what she'd done. He'd been so grateful for everything, the pulling of his hair and the biting of his lip and the ripping off of his clothes and the grinding him under her hips, that she'd been worried he was going to cry. But in the end, she'd been the one to almost cry. John had hugged her like he'd known her his whole life and had been waiting for this exact moment. "Good night," he'd huffed into her ear. Every nerve in her body had pulsed at once.

Then he'd immediately fallen asleep. And strangely, so had she.

Beth's call had broken the spell though. Denise had managed not to wake John, and a half hour after she'd hung up with Beth, she was still lying there perplexed. Why hadn't she left? Why had she stayed in this strange bed?

John breathed deeply and profoundly through his nose, as if he'd never had a single problem in his life. Denise lifted the surprisingly crisp sheet and found his dick lolled over his leg like the tongue of a dog with its head hanging out of a car window. He was much hairier than she would have liked. Chest hair. Shoulder hair. Stomach hair. Zero manscaping. He looked like an unattached strip of Velcro.

She put the sheet down and rolled away from him. In the pale beam of light slipping under the door, she felt alone. Unneeded. She'd fulfilled her duty with John and then with Beth and now she was no one again. The day yawned ahead of her waiting to be filled with meaningful activities. But first she had to pee.

There was no master bathroom in John's bedroom, so she opened the door to the hallway and crept past the shimmering nightlight and into the cramped bathroom. John's towel looked as freshly laundered as his sheets. She rubbed her hand over it as she marveled at his immaculate toilet.

She peed for what felt like an abnormally long time. Then she washed her hands and splashed some water on her face. She sighed at her reflection, then opened the bathroom door and found a little boy standing there.

"Fuck," she said, more of an involuntary sound.

Once the shock reached all of her extremities, she slammed the door closed. Even though Denise had met John at a parent-teacher conference and John had mentioned the babysitter he'd hired for the night and Denise had to wait until the boy was asleep before she could come over, she hadn't expected to see an actual kid in his house. Especially given the fact that she was completely naked and only hours before had been making quite a bit of noise in John's room.

She needed to confront this kid.

Denise grabbed a T-shirt from John's hamper hanging on the back of the door and put it on. It wasn't quite as long as she would have liked so she hunched slightly to get it down to her upper thighs.

She opened the door to find the hallway empty. And the nightlight was off. Denise walked over to the door across from John's room and leaned against it.

"Hey man," she said.

She heard the boy stumble backwards onto the floor.

"Hey," came a small voice from the other side.

"You okay in there?"

"I'm okay." His voice quavered.

"You don't sound fine," Denise said. "Sounds like you're shitting your pants in there."

"I'm not."

"You're not fine? Or you're not shitting your pants?"

A pause. "The second thing."

Denise smiled. Surely this kid had said shit before.

"What's your name?" he said.

"Denise." She pulled on the end of John's t-shirt. "What's yours?"

"Phillip."

Denise tightened her jaw. "You didn't hear us earlier, did you? You know..."

"I didn't even know you were here."

"Same goes for you," she said. "Well, I guess I knew at some point, but I forgot."

"Will you be here later?" he asked. "We have Cocoa Puffs."

"No chance of that. Sorry."

"Okay."

Denise turned to John's room and then spun around again. "Maybe don't tell your dad we talked."

"I won't."

Easy enough. She could still make a clean getaway. She hesitated, slightly hoping he would ask her something else, but he'd gone silent.

She snuck back into John's room and shut the door. Obviously, she should leave right then. But maybe if she nudged John with her elbow as she climbed back into bed, they could have sex one more time before she never, ever, saw him again.

3

Last night, after he saw a completely naked woman in the bathroom, Phillip had picked out a different outfit for the morning just in case he saw her again. He was always prepared for the next day; clothes draped over the back of his desk chair, his backpack loaded with books and ample pencils, his shoes placed neatly at the foot of his bed. But the woman had changed everything. He needed the purple shirt he'd worn to that wedding last summer. And the shiny black shoes.

Phillip had seen her boobs first and that had been so overwhelming that he'd almost missed her "down there" part. The shock had been so sudden, it was like the time Todd Crandell had open palm slapped him on the chest after Phillip had beaten him at tether ball. The woman had frozen in the doorway, posed exactly like a model in one of the magazines in the back of his dad's closet. Had she crawled from one of their pages? Surely that would have made her some kind of a zombie, and the implications of that were terrifying. Her mouth was open so wide his entire brain would have fit inside.

He hoped more than anything that she hadn't left in the night.

It took Phillip three tries to get the buttons lined up on the purple wedding shirt and the shiny black shoes were a little too tight now. He decided at the last second to be casually carrying his most recent math test with the bright red A at the top.

His dad looked up from the table. "What are you wearing, buddy? Are they having a funeral at school?"

"These are wedding clothes," Phillip said and put the test down on the table.

"You planning a trip to Vegas?"

Phillip reached into the cabinet for a bowl. "You think I don't get that joke, but I do."

"Should I be worried then?"

"I just wanted to look nice," Phillip said. Before he sat down, he snuck a look down the hall for any sign of the woman.

"Expecting somebody?"

Phillip wished he wasn't blushing. What even was the point of blushing anyway? He was going to ask Mrs. Clark when he got to school.

His dad must have seen the naked woman too, but he wanted Phillip to bring her up first. Instead of answering, Phillip poured a bowl of Cocoa Puffs. He knew it was silly, but it was hard to stop thinking of the naked woman as if she had actually crawled out of a picture. Her appearance in the house made zero sense and sometimes the least plausible answer was the most likely. He wondered if the naked woman was stuck like that forever or if she would be able to put clothes on. He wasn't sure how it worked for people who came out of magazines.

Phillip's dad poured another bowl of cereal and there was now officially not enough left for the naked woman if she suddenly appeared. Phillip decided not to put milk on his yet just in case.

"What do you want for dinner?" his dad asked. "Since you're all dressed up, do you want to go to that steak place with the all-you-can-eat soft serve machine?"

They usually went there for Phillip's birthday. "Can we really?" he said.

A floorboard creaked in the hallway and Phillip's head snapped to the side quickly enough to pinch a nerve that sent a cascading warmth along the back of his neck. No one was there.

"You saw her, didn't you?" his dad said.

Phillip looked down at his bowl. "Saw who?"

"The lady who was here last night."

"Was she real?" Phillip said.

"I was asking myself the same thing." His dad shook his head and did one of those halfway smiles that showed he was nervous.

"Where did she go?"

His dad shrugged. "She's gone."

Even though it was nice to discover that she was real, the disappointment still pressed down on him like the time Todd Crandell had sat on his chest after Phillip had slipped on some ice on the sidewalk right after Christmas break.

"Will she be back?"

"I doubt it, buddy." His dad stared at him. "She really made an impression on you, huh?"

All at once, Phillip remembered that the naked lady had asked him not to say that he'd spoken to her. "I think we're talking about two different things," he said. "The person I saw was in a dream."

"Look," his dad said. "I know this is strange. And we've never talked about this kind of thing before. I mean, I'm not saying it's going to be a constant occurrence. That I will suddenly start inviting a bunch of ladies over for sleepovers." His dad forced a laugh. "This was an anomaly."

Phillip went ahead and poured his milk. "What's an anomaly?"

"Something that happens that is outside of the normal. For years there have been no sleepovers. Literally none. Which is why I never brought them up as a possibility. And last night there was an anomaly. And now it will probably be years again. So we definitely don't need to make too big of a deal about this."

"You invited her over?" Phillip said.

"Sort of."

"Where did she come from?"

"You mean her place of origin? I don't know. I didn't ask. Maybe that's why I can't get more sleepovers. I don't ask enough questions."

"But she came here just to see you?" Phillip was confused. If the naked woman hadn't climbed out of a magazine, then she was a real person. Where had his dad met a naked woman?

"Don't sound so shocked. Your dad is still a pretty cool guy."

"If you say so," Phillip said.

"You're right," his dad said. "If I have to tell you I'm cool, I'm probably not that cool. Anything else you want to know about a lady sleeping over before we move on to other topics? Like why you brought that Math test out here?"

"What did you and the anomaly do?"

"What do you do on your sleepovers?"

"We usually eat popcorn and drink Coke and watch movies and then see who can be the last one up."

His dad nodded. "That's exactly what we did."

Phillip sat on the curb, his feet throbbing in his black shiny shoes, waiting for his dad to finish getting ready and drive him to school. His dad used to take him and Suz every morning, but Suz had started seventh grade this year and gone off to middle school, leaving Phillip to battle elementary school alone. His new morning ritual involved going out early to talk to Suz before she left. Now that she was doing cheerleading and acting in a play, most days it was the only time Phillip saw her.

Her door opened across the street and there was Suz, tall and glossy, wearing a teal dress the exact color of the water in her aboveground pool. She stomped down the driveway and then over to where Phillip sat on the curb.

"Hey sixth grader," she said as she sat next to him.

"You know you miss it," Phillip said.

"No way. I don't think I could do another year with Mrs. Clark. Anything interesting happening?" She kicked a pebble into the street. "Preferably something funny. I could use a joke this morning."

"My dad had a girl stay over last night."

"Is that the funny part?"

"No. Just strange is all."

"My parents were fighting again."

Phillip had heard them, but he hadn't gone over. He could tell from her expression that she'd waited for him.

"Did you hear them fucking?" she asked.

"What?"

"Your dad and that lady."

"No," Phillip said. "Dad said they ate popcorn and watched a movie."

"Do you even have popcorn at your house?" Suz said.

"No. I don't think so."

"Then they were definitely fucking."

"Maybe she brought the popcorn."

Phillip had a vague idea of what fucking meant and he was absolutely positive his dad would never do it. It was pretty gross. But he had to act casual around Suz now that she was in middle school and she said fucking like it weighed more than other words.

"Then I don't know why she'd stay the night." Suz ran her hand through her curly hair. She trained a faraway glance up to his house.

"My dad doesn't do that."

Suz laughed. "They all do it, Phillip. Sometimes I hear my parents after they have a big fight. Sounds like they're trying to carry a piano upstairs. All this heavy breathing and grunting and shit falling over."

A bee buzzed around Suz's head deciding if it was going to land in her curly hair or not. Phillip shooed it away with his hand.

"Don't piss it off," Suz said. "I don't want to get stung. What are you doing later? You look like you're going to bible camp or something."

Phillip looked down at his purple shirt. He felt silly now, dressing up for the naked lady. "Dad said he'd take me to that place with all-you-can-eat soft serve."

"The steak place? Can I come?"

"I'll ask."

"You don't have to dress up to go there. They'll let in anyone."

The door across the street opened again and there was Suz's dad, his shirt only halfway buttoned. His suit jacket bunched in a ball under his arm.

"Come on, Suz," he growled. He didn't say hello to Phillip, and that's when Phillip knew things were bad.

"Gotta go," she said. "Let me know about dinner. I'd love to get out of the house."

Phillip watched her get into her dad's black convertible and her dad squealed out of the driveway as if he could outrun all of his problems.

The front door to Phillip's house opened and closed quietly behind him. He turned, expecting to see his dad, but no one was there. Before he could decide if that was strange or not, the bee returned, buzzing around Phillip's ear just out of sight. He jumped to his feet and moved toward the house.

Maybe it would be best if he changed clothes before he went to school.

He felt the air shift next to him as he shuffled up the walkway. Like someone had passed him. He stopped and looked into the yard. Everything was still. But he could feel someone staring back at him. The hair on his arms stood up.

Then the bee floated out to exactly where Phillip was staring.

A sharp inhale. The bee dodged back and forth. Its buzzing stopped being exploratory and took on an offensive tone.

"Oh shit," a woman's voice said.

Then suddenly the naked woman appeared where no one had been a moment before. But she was completely clothed now.

They locked eyes.

Then just as quickly, she disappeared from view and Phillip heard footsteps pounding down the sidewalk.

CHAPTER THREE

TREATING THE SYMPTOMS

1

Edna was young again. The skin taut under her arms. No sunspots on her chest and shoulders. She brought her hands to her face and traced her fingertips along her cheekbones. Her mouth opened in expectation.

Nolan appeared in the doorway to her bedroom. He was the broad-shouldered young man she'd married. His arms baked a perpetual golden brown. His golden hair was slightly longer than most men wore their hair back then. The dimple on his right cheek a fissure in his boyish face.

"I heard you needed a handyman," Nolan said in a monotone, as if reading off a cue card.

Edna was supine on the bed. She knew what they were supposed to do. It was why there were hot lights shining on her. And cameras pointing at them both. And eyes watching.

"No," she said. "I don't need a handyman. I need you. I miss you."

Nolan looked confused. Edna had gone off script.

"Don't you need some fixing?" he said, employing a salacious tone he would have never used when he was alive. He waggled his hips. The space between them was suddenly gauzy and indistinct.

"Can you fix me?" she said, but was horrified to discover that her voice now belied all of her sixty-seven years with its airy sing-song quality. She sounded like a librarian. Even though Nolan hadn't aged a day since he'd died, Edna was once again trapped in her fleshy, vein-cluttered body.

Nolan moved toward the bed they once shared.

"No," Edna whispered. "This isn't me. This isn't me."

The cameras pushed closer. The lights got hotter.

"Action," said a director somewhere across the room.

"Not like this," Edna said. "This isn't me. This isn't me. This isn't me."

Edna lurched out of her nightmare and into the nightmare of her life, where for the third time in a month, she'd crapped in the bed.

"Fuck," said the stern schoolteacher who demanded the best of her students.

"Fuck," said the widow who had never slept with another man.

"Fuck," said the old lady with a burgeoning online porn addiction.

Edna yanked the sheets from the mattress, carefully folding the mess inside. She stuffed them into a pillowcase along with her nightgown to carry them down to the laundry room.

And there was Beth coming out of her room like an apparition. She'd forgotten about Beth.

"You need a hand?" Beth said and indicated the pillowcase. She didn't say anything at all about Edna being completely nude.

"I'm just putting it in the car. It's for school," Edna said.

"I can take it. I'm leaving now."

"You're leaving already?" Edna had been so pissed all night but now she suddenly, and desperately, wanted Beth to stay.

"I'm picking up food. Junk stuff. Like Pop-Tarts."

Beth reached out to take the pillowcase.

"I'll do it," Edna said. With her bare thighs rubbing together and the hairs on her arms prickling in a draft, she persisted in her charade, clutching the pillowcase down the stairs. She could feel Beth's eyes on her as they both descended. The more casual Edna acted, the more normal this seemed. Lots of people lived alone and caromed through their homes without a stitch of clothing to cover them. If you don't expect to see someone, then who are you dressing for?

Edna reached the garage, Beth still a few steps behind her. She continued the ruse and deposited the pillowcase onto the floor of the back seat.

"I'll wait to open the garage door," Beth said, the first indication that maybe it was weird to see her mom naked.

"Probably for the best," Edna said and pushed past Beth back into the house. "I'll leave this door unlocked for you."

Edna put on her clothes and looked out the window to make sure Beth was gone. The screen lay crumpled on the floor from when Beth had broken into the house. Oh Beth. The prodigal failure. The master of bad ideas. The deserter of families. It was good to see her, even if it was easier to tell herself it wasn't.

An appliance gurgled somewhere downstairs and it reverberated through the empty house. Being alone again sent a rush of adrenaline coursing through Edna. There were probably hundreds of new videos uploaded to the PornNodule site since she'd last logged on. Maybe she'd find a new video to add to her folder. The perfect one that would precisely fill that oblong empty space hidden behind hardness and sadness and years of being alone. Surrounded by the children in her classes, but utterly bereft of connection. What was the point of being alive if you didn't feel excitement? Or a sense that maybe you were doing something wrong. The thrill of a hidden life.

She turned quickly and a wave of nausea overwhelmed her. She clutched the edge of the bed and waited for it to pass. She squeezed her eyes closed and willed the bile in her stomach to stay where it was.

When it was done, she remembered the pillowcase in the car, and she knew her desktop folder would have to wait.

This time down the stairs, fully clothed, she clutched the railing in case the dizziness returned. She had an appointment with her doctor this morning and she'd mention it to her again. It was probably nothing. Life was littered with nothings, all of them jostling for position in the hopes of accruing weight in Edna's mind. She didn't want to carry around heavy things anymore.

Once Edna was down the stairs she began to move quicker. She wanted to get rid of the pillowcase and get to her computer before Beth returned. Her heart raced like a teenager. Like the way Taylor must have felt all those times he'd snuck out of the house at night.

By the time she got to the garage she was out of breath. She was glad she'd moved the large garbage can inside after Nolan had died. He'd designed a little nook to keep the cans outside but one of Edna's first acts as a widow was moving it into the garage. If she was in charge of the trash now, she was damn well going to do it her way.

She leaned against the station wagon to catch her breath. Maybe it was a good thing she was seeing the doctor today. Even though every time she was there she was unable to believe that she looked as old as the other people inhabiting the waiting room.

Edna took a deep breath and then opened the car and pulled out the pillowcase. It was heavy with her shame.

The garage door sprang to life, the motor suddenly vibrating above like something being demolished. Edna clutched her chest.

"Oh shit," Denise said, also clutching her chest in the exact same way from where she stood in the driveway. "What are you doing lurking around the garage, Mom?" The sun blurred all her edges.

"What are you doing?" Edna managed to wheeze.

"You okay?" Denise stepped forward.

"You nearly scared me to death."

"What's in that pillowcase?" Denise still hadn't come in from the driveway.

"It's something for school," Edna said. And once again the pillowcase was in the car. She shut the door with regret. "You don't just open someone's garage without calling first."

"I never call before I come over," Denise said.

"That's because you don't come over."

"Are you mad at me, Mom? Is there something I'm missing?"

Edna turned toward the door. "Come in and eat something. Or I can write you a check or whatever you need. But I have to get going. I have an appointment."

"Mom."

"Is that not why you're here?"

Denise looked around the garage, clearly trying to muster some better explanation. "Is Beth up?"

"She left."

"Oh," Denise said with a whoosh of air as if Edna had punctured her lung.

"Not for good, unfortunately," Edna said, deciding to add mortar to the wall they'd been erecting between them for years.

"You think she had a job interview?"

Edna laughed.

Denise took a tentative step forward. "Seriously. Are you okay, Mom?"

Edna pictured her pillowcase in the car. A jolt of pain shot through her head and stabbed her behind the right eyeball. She thought of Nolan dressed as a handyman in her dream.

"Nothing I can't fix with a cup of coffee," Edna said and steadied herself for the walk into the house.

2

Hunched in her car in the Jewel parking lot this early in the morning, Beth felt like a fugitive. Or a flasher. Some equally hunched dudes were skulking across the Jewel supermarket parking lot like they were entering Hidden Den, the adult bookstore off the freeway.

She was surprised at the amount of shame that her Pop Tart retrieval task was generating. She'd managed to get herself out of the house and to the grocery store, which was no small feat considering she'd run into her mom. She also had run into all of her mom's bits and pieces. But since her mom didn't seem upset about it, Beth acted like it was normal and she had stared at her mom's ass the whole time she followed her down the stairs. It was shaped like a duffel bag, the same as Beth's own ass. Beth saw an easy trajectory from where she was now to the size of her mom and she wasn't as far away as she'd like to be.

Fran had started Beth's obsession with Basal Metabolic Rates and Total Energy Expenditures. Or as she sadly thought about them now: BMR and TDEE. Her even greater obsession with complete strangers' photographic-weight loss journeys online and their active calories and worst of all, their booty gains. Her mom did not have the type of booty gains she was going for.

Fran, of course, lost forty pounds, and her taut neck muscles and sinewy arms made Beth think of butcher shops and rock striations. Fran was full of compliments for Beth's soft body, but there was an expectation that Beth would eventually stop watching workouts and actually start doing some. She would need to eat the same meals as Fran and exercise all those times a week and miss out on ice cream cakes and refillable popcorn bowls at the movies.

Instead, she dreamed about talking food and continued to pack her duffel bag ass with guilt.

At this point, what did it matter if she walked into the grocery store and bought two boxes of Pop Tarts and nothing else? And who cares if she ate them untoasted in the car before starting her engine? But she was finding it difficult to proceed with the plan. It had nothing to do with her health or that fact that each individual Pop Tart was 200 calories and Kellogg's inexplicably packaged them in pairs in non-resealable bags. So at that point you were guaranteed 400 calories. Which would be nearly half of her allotted calories for the day and she hadn't even had a meal yet.

Something flickered in her peripheral vision and Beth turned in her seat to find a bee lazily bumping against the rear window of her two-door Dodge Neon. Fear shot through her. Irrational and pure. Bees were little death globes with wings that sometimes seemed to be at odds with their own body's plans, vacillating between deliberate and haphazard. Whenever Beth encountered a bee, she became convinced it would be the last thing she'd ever see and she'd be the last thing the bee would ever see, and they would be linked for all of eternity. And if the Universe was circular and Beth had done this before, over and over, then she and this bee would always meet in this moment and there was nothing she could do about it.

Or she could jump out of the car in terror.

"Everything all right?" a startled voice said behind Beth as she slammed the door and ran from her car as if she were in an action movie and the car was about to explode.

Somehow this was less embarrassing than buying Pop Tarts.

"Just a bee," Beth said. "A bee owns my car now. Should I tell him I haven't changed the oil in almost two years?"

The voice laughed and Beth spun to see the source of that musical voice. She saw brown hair loosely tied on top of a woman's head as if a volcano were erupting. Freckles sprinkled across cheeks like confetti. The owner of the voice looked thin. Like dangerously thin.

"Beth Clark?" the woman said, and it gave Beth great pleasure to find that somewhere in the morass of her mind she knew her, because she really, really wanted to talk to her.

"You probably don't recognize me. I'm Renata. From high school. We once smoked cigarettes together and watched Jimmy Franklin crash his mustang into Brenda Marshall's parked car and then drive away."

"Oh shit. Renata," Beth said, the memory coming loose and falling into the proper receptacle in her brain. "What are you doing here?"

"I live here, man. Never left. What are you doing here?"

"I'm back in town," Beth said and pointed at the Jewel store front. "I'm buying Pop Tarts."

Renata laughed again and the resulting smile pulled her skin tight across the bridge of her nose. "I love Pop Tarts. Want to split a bag?"

"Before the bee showed up, I was contemplating why they put two in a bag like that."

"One of life's great mysteries," Renata said. "So. Are you allergic to bee stings?"

"I don't know. My dad was super allergic. A bee killed him, actually."

Renata snorted another laugh and then immediately nipped it. "You're serious, aren't you? I always do that. Laugh at the wrong time."

Beth wasn't sure why she'd told Renata that small bit about her life. She never told anyone that. Not even Fran. "It doesn't sound real, I know. You don't think of people actually dying from a bee sting. You know the bee dies too? So then there's no one left to blame."

"Your dad died of a bee sting but you don't know if you're allergic?"

"I don't want to know. I don't want to get comfortable around bees. I like what we have going. It works for me."

"But now you don't have a car."

"Indeed," said Beth.

"Want me to get it out of there for you?"

"Can I pay you in Pop Tarts?"

"Deal," Renata said as she opened the door to Beth's car and climbed into the back.

3

Kids believed all kinds of ridiculous shit. Like Santa Claus. And the Easter Bunny. And life after death. A kid could tell everyone in his life that he'd seen an invisible woman and no one would think "Hey, I need to follow up on this story."

Specifically, Denise hoped the boy wouldn't tell her mom, because Denise's mom would absolutely believe that story and she'd know exactly who the boy was talking about. Had he somehow told her already? Impossible, of course. But then why had her mom been acting so strangely this morning? It was almost like she knew already. And it was precisely why Denise had waited down the street for her mom to leave and then had began trailing her across town. Denise felt it was very likely that she'd have to explain herself today.

Even though the three of them, Denise and Beth and their brother Taylor, had at some point reached an unspoken agreement to keep what their abilities hidden, Denise used her power quite a bit. Life was a lot simpler for Denise when she used her invisibility to get out of questionable life choices like spending the night with a parent from her mom's classroom, and offsetting financial hiccups by shoplifting food and clothing when she couldn't afford it. She was sure if her brother and sister could come up with practical uses for their talents, they'd use theirs too. She knew Dad would approve.

If only Denise's power was holding on to a job. No matter where she worked, something was always wrong. There might be someone riding her ass that was stupider than her, and Denise would spend her time wondering how that person advanced so far. Or the job description would have failed to mention that she'd have to pick up coffee for the CEO or schedule lunches for someone whose only distinguishing feature was that they had a college degree. Anyone could get one of those. It didn't mean that Denise had to work under them. She had all this potential churning inside of her and nobody had managed to tap into it yet. So surviving meant living off the stipend from her mom and using her true talent, the one she couldn't tell anyone about, to take whatever else she needed.

What if the cascade of mistakes that started from the moment she asked John out to when she let a bee startle her into revealing herself to John's boy somehow brought her current lifestyle to an end. If she had to tell her mom she was fucking parents in her class and stealing from their purses, Denise's arguments for continued help might only elicit a laugh. The dreaded sarcastic mom laugh they all feared.

Her mom turned abruptly in the opposite direction from school, and Denise had to swerve across two lanes of traffic to follow her. It was as if her mom had just been divebombed by a bee as well. She wondered what her mom would think about Denise's bee incident at John's house. It felt like a sign to Denise. Like a message from her dad. Her mom would probably dismiss it outright. There weren't a lot of signs or portents in the real world. But she probably would have wondered why Denise had been so scared. It's not like two people in the same family were going to die from bee stings. That would be ludicrous.

Denise wasn't sure where she expected her mom to go, but she was surprised when she pulled into the sparkling new medical complex along the frontage road of the freeway. Denise parked a few rows away and shut off her engine.

A moment later, her mom was on the move, shuffling toward the front of the medical complex. Denise flexed that imaginary muscle, and now invisible, hurried out of the car. She slipped into the building behind a bald man with a severe rash on his face, conscious to try not to interact with too many things in the world. People tended to notice when doors opened on their own.

Her mom got into the elevator. Denise stepped in quickly, watched her mother press the button for the third floor, and then hopped out. The stairs were safer.

There were no other people in the stairwell, which was a good thing because her every invisible step echoed in waves of sound. She opened the door for the third floor very slowly, peeking out to make sure no one was standing on the other side. When she was sure the coast was clear, she pushed out into the hallway. The door closed behind her.

Her mom had already left the elevator and must have chosen one of two doors at the far end of the hall. If not, she would have walked right past Denise as she was trying to exit the stairwell.

Denise tiptoed to the end of the hall and put her ear to the first door. It swung open and an emaciated man barreled into the hallway. Denise was so startled that she almost let go of her invisibility muscle again. But she lurched backward just in time, letting the man pass, and then stumbled into the tiny waiting room. She was losing her touch.

There was her mom idly rifling through a magazine.

A door across the room opened with a hissing noise and a young man in scrubs called out "Edna Clark."

"I just sat down," Denise's mom said. "I hadn't even settled on an article yet."

The young man in scrubs gave her a wan smile. "So sorry. Hopefully you can be grateful for our punctuality."

Her mom dropped the magazine with a huff and Denise followed her into another hallway. The young man led them to a stuffy examination room. Denise jammed herself into the corner to avoid them.

"The doctor will be right with you," the young man said. Denise's mom leaned onto the crinkling white paper on the examination table.

"I won't get too comfortable," her mom said.

Denise tried not to breathe. Not to move. To slow the rhythms of her body.

Her mom was perfectly still too. Denise hadn't been this close to her in years. She and Beth looked so much alike.

The door opened and the doctor entered, slightly yellowed, as if somewhere along the line someone had adjusted her tint and never returned it to normal. She wore a wrinkled white coat and a terribly grim expression. She held a sheaf of papers.

She shut the door and stared at Denise's mom.

"You're making me uncomfortable," Denise's mom said.

"When you were here last we did that scan. I didn't expect to find anything, but you were complaining of dizziness..." She waved the papers around as if they could conjure a picture of that past appointment.

Denise's mom narrowed her eyes then let out a dry laugh. "I'm dying, aren't I, Dr. Green? It's in my brain."

Dr. Green hesitated, then nodded. "It's called a glioblastoma."

"How long do I have?"

"Maybe eight months," Dr. Green said. "And that's with aggressive treatment."

"I don't want treatment. I'd like to finish this last month of school and go out with dignity."

Dr Green dropped her voice. "This is a difficult decision. Take your time. Talk to your family. In the mean time, I wouldn't advise you to continue teaching. There's a high risk of seizure. This thing is growing, pressing against your frontal lobe. It can affect your memory and even your personality. Your students may not recognize you anymore."

"Can we treat those symptoms?"

"I can give you a corticosteroid shot that will lower intracranial pressure, decreasing headaches and alleviating some pain."

"I'll take it."

"Edna, I've known you a long time." Dr. Green had tears in her eyes. "Let's not just talk about this in clinical terms. Can we talk like friends? I want to talk about how you are as well as how you're feeling. I want to help you and your family through this difficult time, whatever you decide to do."

"My mind is made up, Dr. Green. Schedule that shot. And if you tell any of my children, I'll come after your medical license. This is between us."

"Of course, Edna, if those are your wishes. But you need to tell your children. They need to know so they can be there for you."

"I just want to finish the school year and then slip out of memory."

Dr. Green sighed. "Wait here. I'll be back." She gave Denise's mom a pained look and left the room.

Denise's mom turned and stared directly where Denise was standing.

"I know you're there, Denise. You keep this to yourself. I know I can count on you. Otherwise, I won't put you in my will."

CHAPTER FOUR

HIDING THE FEELINGS

1

"She drove away and no one ever saw him again." Todd Crandell lowered his eyebrows, expanding his already massive forehead, and leered at Phillip. Suz would think he was crazy for spending any time with someone she had always called a blowhard and a bully wannabe.

But Phillip kept an eye on Todd Crandell's hands, aware that they could make contact with any part of Phillip's body with no warning. "Why would they keep letting Mrs. Clark teach here if she kidnapped a kid?"

Todd Crandell's eyes opened wide now, his eyebrows shooting up to his hairline. "Because nobody saw. Nobody could prove anything."

"So there was an investigation?" Phillip said. "They looked into this?"

Todd Crandell's left hand rocketed suddenly into Phillip's shoulder and nearly twisted him off balance. "Of course they did."

"And the boy is still missing?" Somehow said without wincing.

"Wouldn't be a mystery if he wasn't." Todd Crandell smiled, assured that he'd at least hooked Phillip slightly. Which he had.

"Why did he get into the back of Mrs. Clark's car?"

"It's not for us to understand the actions of a person with diminished brain capacity," Todd Crandell said.

"He had something wrong with him?" Phillip said, suddenly feeling sorry for this boy.

"I meant that he's a moron."

Phillip and Todd Crandell were standing near the water fountain outside the boys' bathroom. Their class had been combined with Mr. Scully's because Mrs. Clark hadn't shown up that morning. Todd Crandell was convinced it was because she'd been taken to jail for her past crime of kidnapping a boy in broad daylight. Right here from school.

To stall their return to Mr. Scully's overcrowded room, Phillip and Todd Crandell were taking turns drinking out of the water fountain. Even though they were in sixth grade, the school still made the students go in pairs to the bathroom.

"He got into the car on his own? She didn't drag him?" Phillip said. He was aware of his own gullibility. And susceptibility. He wanted magic and mystery in the world and he wasn't convinced that all of it didn't exist. He'd give anything a chance. Literally anything.

Todd Crandell shrugged and took a big slurp of water. "Maybe Mrs. Clark told him she'd take him for ice cream. Or the movies. Or a petting zoo. The point here is no one knows. It's unsolved."

Todd Crandell was a reluctant bully. He had the physique and the brutishness. He had an emotional physicality that led every one of his moods to be broadcast with bodily contact. But he was also bright. Definitely the smartest kid Phillip knew. They were almost friends. Two boys with enough knowledge to get in trouble who sometimes gravitated toward each other for mental stimulation and other times for Todd Crandell to brutalize Phillip in some way that would absolutely scar. Phillip was fairly sure that Suz had a crush on him, and that burned a nerve hidden somewhere deep in his chest.

"What do you think became of him?" Phillip leaned toward the water fountain. It was hard to imagine Mrs. Clark kidnapping someone. It was even harder to imagine her hurting him in some way. But Phillip was willing to give some fancy to this flight.

The metal door to the teacher parking lot banged open and there was Mrs. Clark with so much hazy sunlight behind her she looked as if she were being erased.

Phillip and Todd Crandell stared at her. She stared back at them. Phillip was unable to move, his hand stuck on the water fountain button, the water making a pleasant bubbling sound as it swirled into the drain.

The metal door began to close slowly behind Mrs. Clark and as the sun became obscured, her features began to fill in.

Even with a hall pass for the bathroom and no history of delinquent behavior, Phillip was terrified. Could Mrs. Clark manage to grab both of them and hurl them into her car? Would their punishment for loitering be an inclusion into the annals of school lore? Were they about to be kidnapped?

The door closed with a heavy bump and Mrs. Clark jumped forward. "Boo!" she called and her voice echoed in the hallway.

Both Phillip and Todd Crandell flinched, and Mrs. Clark cackled.

"You trying to dwindle the county's water supply, Phillip?" Mrs. Clark said as she approached the boys with a slight stoop to her shoulders.

Phillip blushed, which reminded him that he had planned to ask Mrs. Clark today why people blushed in the first place, and he removed his hand from the water fountain button.

"No ma'am," Phillip said.

"I assume you have a hall pass and everything is on the up and up here?"

Phillip and Todd Crandell nodded.

"Carry on then," she said and shuffled past them, her shoes emitting tiny squeaks on the polished floor.

"There goes your theory," Phillip said.

"It's not a theory if we prove it," Todd Crandell said.

Phillip took another sip from the water fountain. His mouth had actually dried in the momentary terror he'd felt. "How do you plan to do that?"

"That's where you come in," Todd Crandell said. "You're going to solve the mystery."

"Really?"

"You're going to get into her car and hide yourself away before she leaves for the day. Then she'll drive home and you're going to sneak into her house and find clues."

"That's not happening." To emphasize his point, Phillip took a drink from the cold-water fountain. One eye still on Todd Crandell's hands.

"Sure it is. You scared or something?"

"If you want to know so bad," Phillip said, "why don't you sneak into her car?"

"Look at me, man. I'm huge. There's no way I could hide in the back of the car without her seeing me. Try using your brain every once in a while then look at yourself in the mirror. You're like a broom handle. Like a twig that blew into her car. You crouch down on the floor in the back and she'd never see you."

The words "never see you" brought back the image of the woman appearing and disappearing in front of his eyes that morning. Brought back the fact that she must have been real because she'd been scared of a bee. She'd cursed loudly. Phillip had heard her frantically retreating footsteps. But now, a few hours since the incident, it was harder to believe he'd seen her than it was to believe Mrs. Clark kidnapped a boy. Or that a naked woman could crawl from the pages of a magazine. The very idea of proof muddied everything.

He wondered what Todd Crandell would think if Phillip countered this tall tale with a tale of his own. About an invisible woman. But Phillip knew Todd Crandell wouldn't believe him. Not even Suz would believe him, but that wouldn't stop him from telling her later.

"I'll think about it," Phillip said.

Todd Crandell smiled. "I knew I liked you."

They began their slow walk to class.

"Have you seen Suz lately?" Todd Crandell asked.

Phillip didn't like the way that sounded at all.

2

John was a terrible father. He knew it with blazing certainty. The same way he knew that his own father was terrible. And his father's father. And his father's father's father. John came from a long line of terrible fathers who manifested failure and who blamed everyone but themselves. John's solution to his faulty genetics was an earnest attempt at hiding his deficiency.

Perhaps no one would notice John was bad at parenthood if he drove Phillip to school every day and picked him up after. Or if John prepared Phillip's favorite sandwich (tuna fish) every night and wrapped it in tinfoil and put it in a brown bag with a Ziploc full of potato chips and three Oreo cookies and placed it on the top shelf of the refrigerator for Phillip to grab in the morning. One surefire way John discovered to divert attention from his ineptitude was ensuring Phillip always had a haircut and clothes that fit perfectly. If anyone asked, John sat with Phillip in the evenings and helped him with his homework and he took an interest in everything that interested his son. Another successful smokescreen was that he and Phillip did Friday movie nights and Sunday ice cream excursions and went to library every few weeks to get stacks of books. But the icing on the diversionary tactics cake was that John answered any question, no matter how tough or probing, that Phillip had about the mother who had abandoned him before he'd developed the ability to form lasting memories.

One thing John never did was make time for new relationships. He had a few friends from high school who had stuck with him through his rushed marriage to Molly, the birth of Phillip, and then Molly's subsequent abrupt exit. But when it became clear that he wasn't going to continue playing video games online or contribute to the ongoing conversations where they over-analyzed Marvel movies, the Star Wars universe, and the oeuvres of independent film directors, John was relegated to calls on birthdays and holidays and periodic check-ins. Invitations were scarce. He met no new people. The scope of John's world shrunk to the size and shape of his preternaturally smart son who was constantly staring at him with his bulging brown eyes as if one day John was going to explain everything and Phillip damn well wasn't going to miss it.

Every morning he had to fight the urge to stop Phillip from getting out of the car. John watched him scuttle up the cement steps toward the gaping maw of the school with a creeping sense of dread. It was as if the school were a hungry beast that would swallow Phillip in one gulp and John would never see him again. The moment Phillip got out of the car, the tenuous thread that connected them was severed, and John had to wait seven hours to see if Phillip survived without him.

He always did.

John pushed through the glass doors into the lobby twenty minutes late. Again. The office smelled like the microwave pancakes Kate ate every morning; the brown sugar like impending death. The pancakes had surely been consumed by now, but the stink would be there until lunchtime. At which point Kate would heat up Indian food or something comparably aromatic. And the moment that scent dissipated, she'd make popcorn.

"Nice of you to show up," Kate said. Her purple lipstick made her seem much kinder than she actually was.

"Thank you," John said.

She shook her head and dismissed him with a wave. She was the lowest on the totem pole, but everyone was scared of her disdain. Even the lawyers deferred to her. But John tended to poke at her a little.

"When I was at the grocery store, they were out of those brown sugar pancakes. I bet you have quite the stock at home."

"Har dee har har," she said. That meant fuck you in Kate's world, but she'd never say it.

John stepped around Kate's desk and toward the bank of three cubicles. His was in the middle, and even though John had worked there for more than ten years, he'd resisted putting up anything personal. Jobs never seemed permanent until they were. His one concession was that each year he affixed Phillip's new school photo to the edge of his computer. If John scanned his eyes along them, it was like a flipbook of Phillip getting more and more comfortable in his skin. John powered on his computer and placed his bag on the gleaming white desktop before walking toward Brad Green's office.

Brad Green was his boss. A lawyer to be exact. And John was his assistant.

The first thing Brad Green wanted people to know about him was that he was a huge Raiders fan. He had jerseys framed on the wall and signed footballs and ticket stubs and bobble heads. His office looked like a thirteen-year-old boy's bedroom.

Brad liked things a particular way and it was John's duty to make sure that happened. He wanted his blinds opened and his small desk lamp snapped on before he arrived. He wanted a printed copy of the day's schedule placed on his chair. And that's just the normal stuff. John had to make sure he had three pens, no more, no less, in the black plastic holder on his desk. He wanted the newspaper opened to the sports section on his leather couch. But worst of all, he wanted John to log on to his computer and email his wife. John pretended like he was Brad, and he told her he'd made it to work safely. John had no idea where Brad actually went in the morning, and he'd never ask him.

John had nightmares about some sort of state-mandated Bring Your Son To Work Day where Phillip is forced to accompany him to the law offices and he sees how demeaning John's job is. Phillip watches him answer phones, assemble court documents and schedule Brad Green's lunches. Then, at the end of the day, he's shown a copy of John's paycheck. That might be enough to shred the last remaining respect Phillip might have had for him.

John finished in Brad's office and returned to his cubicle and immediately started thinking about Denise. He didn't know her last name or her phone number, but he knew she had a mole on her hip. Calluses on her heels. A slightly sour smell on her breath. He'd give anything to find her at his house when he got home tonight. He could properly introduce her to Phillip. Stop acting like his happiness was on hold. But he knew he wouldn't see her again. No matter how many parent-teacher conferences he attended. There had been a small rip in the fabric of the universe which closed behind her the moment she'd stepped back through it. To her own timeline. Her own problems. Her own life.

Brad walked in at quarter to eleven. He pointed at John, his hand shaped like a gun, and flashed his teeth. John hated when he did that. He felt demeaned enough, he didn't need Brad shooting him on top of everything else.

"Johnny boy," he said. John hated that too. Come to think of it, there wasn't much he liked about Brad Green, Esq. "Just got off the phone with opposing council. Those cocksuckers think they have me over the table, balls deep." John had been there long enough to know that Brad equated everything to getting fucked in the ass.

Instead of asking John to follow him into his office, Brad went in alone and sat down at his desk. Then he buzzed John's phone.

Matt in the next cubicle chuckled, his headset permanently attached to his narrow skull. He shook his head as if he knew something John didn't. Like everyone was in on a private joke except him.

"What's so funny?" John said.

Matt shrugged, never once making eye contact.

John knocked softly on Brad Green's door, partially hoping he wouldn't hear.

"Come in," Brad said. "Shut the door after you." He motioned to a chair across from him. With all his Raiders paraphernalia, it felt like the walls were going to crumble on top of them both.

Brad sighed and leaned forward, as if he'd been watching gangster movies non-stop in his spare time. "I'm just going to throw it out there. You're fired."

The words that set John free from this misery also dealt a mortal blow. Without this job, how would he support Phillip? "Please don't do this to me," John said. "I'll change whatever you need me to change."

"It's been decided already."

"By who?" John said.

"Me. I'm the boss, John. I just do what I want."

"I've been here eight years."

"I know."

John stopped all regularly scheduled breathing, which accounted for the tiny spots that were exploding in the air between them. "Just tell me why."

Brad leaned back and put his hands behind his head. "Company policy states that I can fire you at any time without warning. With no explanation. You agreed to that when you started here."

"But that's not how you treat people."

Brad sighed. "You and me. We aren't equals, John."

"Is that so?" John rubbed his tongue on the top of his mouth to induce saliva.

"I have a law degree. And you have a degree to be my bitch."

If John knew how to kill a man with his bare hands, he'd have launched across the desk, sending Raiders paraphernalia flying everywhere. Maybe he would have jammed one of those stupid pennants into Brad's eye.

Brad gritted his teeth and sucked in air. He knew he'd gone too far. "I appreciate all your hard work over the years. I do." He stuck out his hand.

John stared at it. The proffered hand. "I hate everything about you," he said.

"I know you do, John," Brad said with a smile. "And it's my pleasure to never see you again."

Brad gave up on the handshake. He clasped his hands together and tilted his head to the left. He seemed to be having a hard time determining which loathsome pose to adopt. He'd probably been waiting for this day for years.

"When is my last day?" John asked.

"Today works for me."

John turned to leave, and Brad cleared his throat. "I'm sorry," he said.

Did Brad Green apologize? It didn't seem possible.

Brad cleared his throat again. "I meant to have you get me a cup of coffee before you came in here. Do you mind?"

John walked out of his office, past the cubicles, past Matt, past Karen, past the microwave, and out the door for the last time.

He was screwed.

3

"This is creepy," Renata said. "It's like a time machine to the worst time of my life."

Beth looked at her bedroom and shrugged. "I don't know. It gives me some comfort. Like eating your favorite food or watching your favorite movie."

Renata flushed red which Beth enjoyed seeing. Very much.

"Don't get me wrong," Renata said. "I think it's cool to be here. I would have totally come over if you'd invited me in high school. I would have pretended to know what all these movies are. I sort of dreamed of what your room looked like."

"Ta da," Beth said. "In that case, it is a time machine. It's exactly as it was."

"But now that I'm here, I'm not going to pretend to know these movies, though, if that's okay."

"I can quote them verbatim," Beth said because she had watched Akira and Princess Mononoke and Ghost in the Shell non-stop when she'd lived in her apartment in the city. It had bugged Fran in those early days when she'd first started staying through the night that Beth used anime as white noise.

"You ever hear of that torture technique where they play prisoners the same song over and over and over?" Fran had said. "It's usually something grating. Like a metal song."

"If you feel tortured, don't come over anymore," Beth had said, but Fran had returned many more times after that. She'd even once shown up with a DVD of the Tom Hanks movie You've Got Mail, presumably to replace the droning anime, but Beth had laughed so hard she'd hurt Fran's feelings. Turns out Fran loved hetero romantic comedies, especially ones with Tom Hanks. Beth eventually watched them all. Except the volcano one.

Renata turned to her. "I've insulted your room and admitted how lame and lonely I was when we were in school. Maybe I've embarrassed myself enough for one day?"

With Renata in her childhood room, something fluttered in the space between Beth's stomach and bladder and she decided not to worry about the future. The future was Schrödinger's cat. In the unknown future, Beth was both alive and dead. She was a failure and a success. She was in love and in pain.

Then her phone rang. Beth knew it was Fran. She knew she should answer but she was stretched across a chasm. At one end was the life she had abandoned. At the other was a world of new possibilities. And absolutely anything, truly anything, could happen now that Renata was looking at her sheepishly. Waiting for Beth to say it was okay. That she wasn't offended. That it was okay for her to stay.

Beth stepped backwards out of the room. She needed a minute. She wasn't ready to decide. The phone rang again.

"You okay?" Renata said. "Is there a bee?"

Beth took another step back, and Renata followed her into the hallway.

"Do you want me to go?" Renata said as she reached out toward Beth.

Beth stepped back once more.

"Not yet. No. I don't know."

And then Beth fell down the stairs.

CHAPTER FIVE

EXPERIENCING THE PAIN

1

Somewhere in Denise's brain there was a synapse firing. The message it was trying to convey was that her mom was dying. But the surrounding synapses were releasing neurotransmitters containing conflicting messages which were sowing much confusion and doubt. Denise had misheard. That was certainly an option, but unlikely. It was much more likely that the doctor was mistaken. Another round of tests would confirm that the tumor was actually just a smudge on the x-ray. Or in a sick comedy of errors, her mom's x-ray had been switched with another patient. There was even a small chance that her mom had known Denise would follow her and she had set up the whole doctor visit to fuck with her. But if it was real and there really was a glioblastoma living in her mom's skull, then of course Dr. Green would save her. That was obvious.

Denise had sat in her car for over an hour after leaving Dr. Green's office. She'd watched her mom drive away and then her central nervous system had shut down and she'd slumped in her seat as stranger after stranger entered the medical offices, some of them surely receiving word that their days on earth were coming to an end as well. Everybody realizes they can't live forever, but nobody wants to die right now, Denise thought. Right now is a terrible time to die.

When Denise's body began whirring again, she started her car and drove to the elementary school. There was her mom's car in the parking lot, a hazy line along the side where snow and salt had been hurled by its tires over a long winter. There was the spot, just under the monkey bars, where Denise had let

Nathan Robertson kiss her on the lips in sixth grade. If she squinted, she could see her dad smoking a cigarette under the sprawling willow tree outside the front doors where he had waited for her every afternoon. Even in death he was an imposing figure, broad shouldered and staggeringly tall. But now, looking at him from a future he would never see, Denise realized he was a bit rakish as well, unsettling people just enough to be left alone most of the time. No one ever told him he couldn't smoke out there.

After Taylor had started kindergarten, when Denise was in fourth grade and Beth had been in sixth, Taylor would ride on their dad's shoulders to where their dad had parked on the street away from the commotion of the pick-up zone. Her dad had been such a large presence that he had dwarfed everyone else. No, that wasn't exactly right. It was like no other students or their families were there. It was just the three of them and their dad. Sometimes, Denise even had a hard time finding her mom in her memories.

Taylor had been closest to their dad and had taken his loss the hardest. He'd spent his formative years attempting to be a facsimile of the larger-than-life man, taking stories he'd heard from their mom about their dad in his youth and playing them out. He started smoking before he could drive and regarded school as a place that was trying to crush him. He managed to become withdrawn while trying very hard to be aloof. His attempts at being acerbic came off as whiny. But when he'd learned that their dad had been a decent bass player, he took to it with a fervor that he had never shown before. Music had saved him.

If only there had been some way to save their dad. It seemed impossible then that he would die, and it seemed impossible now. He'd been more cavalier about his power. Stronger than the strongest strongman. He could pull a small tree from the ground with all its roots still attached. He could stop a moving car. He could protect their family from anything.

But a bee. A lousy bumbling bee brought him down.

Denise thought of the bee from this morning. No wonder it was so easy for people to believe in something bigger than the world they could see. With little or no imagination, she could convince herself that the bee that had targeted her was some kind of sign. Maybe her dad telling her that John was a good guy, which he was. Denise knew that deep inside. Better than she deserved. Maybe her dad trying to get her to go back inside. To reveal herself.

Or if she wanted, she could spin it another way. The bee was telling her she'd made a horrible mistake. Her father, somehow still intact in another realm, was sending bee messengers to warn her about her actions. The risk associated with using her power. His displeasure with her thievery. Because she'd of course taken something from John's house. A little something to remember him by. And she would remember him fondly when she used all the cash he'd had in his wallet to buy dinner for herself tonight.

Or maybe, just maybe, the bee was just a bee. And her mom was dying. And Beth was back in their lives. And now Denise needed Taylor here too. If they were all together, they could figure out what to do. Denise couldn't do it on her own.

She pulled out her phone to call Taylor and it sprang to life in her hands, Beth's name on the display. She wouldn't tell Beth just yet.

"I tried to see you this morning," Denise said.

"After all the dreams, I broke down and bought Pop-Tarts," Beth said, her voice weak. Maybe she knew about their mom already.

"Is everything okay? Did something happen?" Denise gripped the steering wheel of her parked car.

"Everything's fine. What are you up to?"

Something was off. Beth wasn't chatty.

"Mom is dying," Denise said. Whoops.

"Oh."

A class exploded from the school doors and out onto the playground. Colorful bursts of light like a concussion.

"You mean eventually? Or like, right now?" Beth's voice still seemed diminished, as if talking was an effort.

"In between right now and eventually."

"Soon?"

"Yeah, soon. I wasn't supposed to tell you."

"Why did you?"

"I didn't think it was fair that I was the only one who knew."

"Are you sad?" Beth said.

"Yes. Aren't you?"

"Definitely. Really sad."

The children scattered across the playground.

"I'm in the hospital, and I was hoping you could pick me up," Beth said.

"Are you dying too?"

"Not for a long, long time," Beth said.

"Okay then. I'll pick you up."

"What if I was dying?"

"I would have left you at the hospital. I can't handle that kind of energy."

Beth laughed. "Fair enough."

2

Edna stared at her class. Row after row of rumpled, foul-smelling sixth graders. A Petri dish of every cold and flu known to man. Bags of mucus and farts and earwax. Replicas of their parents' insecurities and failings. But she loved each and every one of them from the moment they appeared in the Fall to the last day of school in the Spring. They were her life. And one day, they too would die and mesh with the Earth, thus speeding along the total annihilation of her memory. She wouldn't be the one to tell them though. Let them learn that on their own.

About an hour ago, Edna had looked out the window to find that Denise had finally driven away, but she could still feel her presence looming. Now that she thought about it, that was the perfect way to describe Denise. She had been looming over Edna for years. Constantly wanting and needing and prying. The children in her class could ask her for anything, but her own children's wants and desires had become a burden after Nolan had died.

It had been a long time since she'd caught Denise spying. Not since high school. As far as Edna knew, none of her children used their gifts anymore. They'd consigned themselves to obscurity just like the rare talented children who had passed through her classroom over the years. The most gifted ones did everything they could to not stand out. Edna would run into these previously talented former students at WalMart as adults. They had abandoned their specialness. They were as gray as a snowy day. If Nolan hadn't died, things might have been different, but as it turned out, her own children had sanded their edges too. When Edna thought about the opportunities that her three remarkable children had wasted, her chest tightened. She could see Nolan's disappointed face. His legacy stalled.

"Mrs. Clark?"

A tiny pre-pubescent voice brought her back to the classroom where she found Phillip standing on the other side of her horribly dented metal desk.

"Glad to see you aren't sneaking around the halls anymore," she said.

Phillip smiled shyly.

"What would have happened if we never came back?"

"They'd probably send a search party. Bloodhounds. Helicopters. GPS trackers. They'd find you."

"What if they didn't though?"

Edna shook her head gravely. "They'd eventually give up the search. Some people would cry. I might a little. You're a good speller." She smiled at him. "And everybody would talk about you in whispers after that. You'd be a school legend. A tale about what could happen if you abuse your hall pass."

Phillip seemed frustrated. Maybe he was trying to tell her something. Some code that only a sixth-grade boy would know.

"Is there a problem, Phillip?" she said. "Something you're trying to tell me?"

He hung his head. "No."

"Everything okay at home?"

He nodded quickly. "Yes. It's great."

"Well, you know you can always talk to me," she said. Until, of course, she wasn't around anymore.

"I know."

"So, do you have a question?"

"Actually," he said, "why do people blush?"

"When you do something silly, all of your blood and organs get so embarrassed to be around you that they try to shoot out of your body."

"Is that true?"

"Of course it's true. I'm a teacher."

It wasn't until she pushed through the door at the end of the day that the dearth of her remaining time on Earth settled in. She was a dying woman now, and not just in the abstract. She looked out across the parking lot that she'd seen thousands of times, listened to the sound of the door squeaking, felt the pavement under her shoes, and she wrapped little bows around it all. Memories to be savored. But she wasn't retiring. She wasn't going to be thinking back on these days fondly. She was going to be dead. There would be no more happy memories. No more bad memories. No more anything. The accumulation of experiences suddenly pointless. Banal. Stupid.

Then the door squeaked open behind her and she knew, just knew without a doubt, it was Hank.

"Hey lady," he said as he caught up to her. He wore an ill-fitting brown blazer that hunched awkwardly over his knobby shoulders. In the twenty years they'd worked together, Edna had watched him shrink until the skin stretched across his cheekbones. He was dying too, just a little more slowly.

"Thanks for watching my class this morning," Edna said, hiding her face from him. He would know she was upset.

"Any time," he said, leaning forward as he walked, hoping to catch her eye. "You alright?"

"Yes. Fine. Like always." Unfortunately, this wouldn't be the first time Hank had seen her out of character. She should have never told him that she'd lost her husband. Now Hank thought they were part of some goddamn widows' club.

"I'm having a hard time myself today," he said. "It doesn't get easier, does it?"

"It doesn't. But platitudes don't get any platitudiner."

"Ouch."

Hank slowed his gait, giving Edna a moment to wipe her eyes.

"Being a good friend means I know when you want to talk and when you don't," he said. "I get angry myself sometimes."

Edna stopped and turned toward him. "I'm sorry, Hank. It just feels sometimes that there is no way to heal. That all of our sadness and ache is pointless."

"It's not pointless," Hank said, leaning toward her. She smelled his medicinal aftershave. "Pointless would be letting them go as if they were never here. We are the point."

Edna forced a smile. "Let's not get lost in mumbo jumbo. But I hear you."

"Today is Monica's death anniversary," Hank said.

Oh fuck.

"I told you last year. You should take this day off from work," Edna said.

"Then I would just feel sorry for myself all day. It's better to be with the kids."

"Yes. They do offer solace, don't they? I'm sure Monica approves of whatever you decide to do today." She looked into Hank's sad, sad eyes. She knew her own eyes were an equal match. "I should get going. Take care of yourself, Hank."

He put his warm hand on her elbow. She stopped, her breath hovering in her throat. A current entered her body, pulsing through her arm and into her chest. She had forgotten how good it felt to be touched.

"I have an idea," he said. "Why don't we get lunch this weekend? Saturday maybe?"

She opened her mouth to respond but a tiny sob came out.

"Edna?"

Her brain began to crack along its seams. She thought of the blood pulsing through her veins. The whirring of her nervous system. The acids in her stomach. All of the functions that would cease forever. Then there was Nolan. Not how he actually was, but how he was in the dream. She wanted to push him away. She wanted to pound on his chest and slap his face and yell every ugly word she could muster. They were going to be in oblivion together without ever being aware of each other again.

Hank steadied her as she swayed on her feet. She leaned onto his shoulder. Then she reached down and grabbed his crotch.

His surprised cock shifted from where it had been pressed against his left leg and heat radiated from his thick ball sack.

Hank gasped but didn't move. She wrapped her fingers as best as she could around his shaft, his trousers bunching in her hand.

"Think about that lunch," he said as he pulled away from her. Edna's outstretched hand tingled and she held it there until her shoulder ached.

She watched him get into his station wagon before the full force of the embarrassment hit her. She almost collapsed right there on the ground and commenced departing from her body.

Instead, Edna approximated running to her car. She climbed in quickly, hoping that if anyone had seen her attempt to turn her life into a pornographic film, he or she would be unable to recognize her.

Then she drove cautiously and slowly out of the school parking lot in case any children were around.

She sped through town, luckily avoiding most traffic lights. Her head felt heavy. Not just with shame of what she'd done. But it was as if she could feel the tumor itself. The solidity of it. The gravity.

Then she rolled to a stop in her driveway and closed her eyes, instantly sucked inward. Propelled through her sinuses and into her spongy brain. The tumor lay there, curled like a fetus in the hollow above her forehead. Throbbing and bristling with power. Edna stared with awe at the agent of her destruction.

"I'm coming for you," the glioblastoma said softly.

"Get out of my head, and I'll let you live," Edna said without conviction.

"Too bad that I," chortled the tumor, "can't make the same promise to you."

She opened her eyes and caught a movement in the rearview mirror. A sharp intake of breath. She leaned over the seat and there was Phillip tucked onto the floor looking up at her. Perhaps she should have been more shocked, but not much surprised her anymore.

"What are you doing?"

"Investigating," he said in a whisper.

"And it involves stowing away in my car?"

He nodded. "What's in that pillowcase?"

On the floor next to him was the pillowcase from that morning. As if sensing her attention, an angry smell wafted into the front seat. How had she forgotten that?

Edna flushed. "Sometimes the answer is as obvious as it seems."

He blinked up at her.

"It's shit, Phillip. It's a pillowcase with shit in it."

"Do you have a dog?"

Edna couldn't stop a dry laugh from heaving out of her. She opened the garage, hoisted the offending pillowcase over the seat, and stumbled out of the car. Phillip's eyes peered through the back window as she lifted the lid for the can and tossed the pillowcase inside. In case Beth were to somehow stumble upon it, she buried it at the bottom, her shame now covered by boxes of microwave meals and cans of pop. She rubbed her eyes with the balls of her hands and sighed.

"You need to call your dad," she said to Phillip, still cowering in the back seat.

He shook his head.

"Open the door and come inside. I'm not going to kidnap you."

Phillip hurried out of the car like a small rodent. Edna gave him her patented pursed smile.

"I don't know my dad's number," Phillip said.

"How are all you children going to live in the big bad world when you can't hold on to any knowledge?"

"I've tried. I even made a song out of it. But the harder I try to remember the easier it is to forget."

"That's bad news," Edna said.

Phillip thought for a moment. "I know my mom's number though. Dad has it saved on his phone and I memorized it."

"Perfect," Edna said. "Let's call her." Only a quick thought as to why that number was so much easier to retain.

He hesitated, his right hand clutching the fingers of his left hand like he was milking a cow. "I've never met her," he said.

Edna opened the door into the house. "Today is as good as any."

3

Molly's needs were modest. For starters, she didn't want to work. No more carrying trays of fried food to ungrateful college students. No more reciting the list of house beers while wearing a tight shirt and push-up bra. She never again wanted to feel that permeating hatred when someone didn't leave a tip. She wanted a life where she didn't have to count on the generosity of strangers.

As soon as she got work out of the way, she would concentrate on getting ten hours of uninterrupted sleep a night. She wanted a king-sized bed so she could lie on her back and stretch her arms out to her side and spread her feet wide. She'd create a snow angel in her 1,000-thread-count sheets.

She never wanted to drive in traffic again, so it would be best if she had a driver. Molly could watch a movie in the backseat of a Lincoln Town Car while they crept down the 405 Or she could study her lines for an audition. In the spare time she would now be accumulating, she could do local theater or join an improv group in addition to a recurring role on a TV show.

She also wanted a personal trainer and two walk-in closets. One for clothes and one for shoes. She wanted to skip the lines at nightclubs. She never wanted to see a utility bill again.

These were all her dreams. And then her roommate went out and achieved them. All she had to do was marry a rich, moderately lecherous old man with visible veins on his face.

She told Molly the name of the app where she'd met him while she'd packed her things and left Molly with both halves of the split rent.

So now Molly was online dating.

And that's how she found herself sitting in traffic on the 405, exhausted after working a double yesterday, fighting her way down to Santa Monica while running her audition monologue even though she had no upcoming auditions and her agent had dumped her right before pilot season, her neck aching from sleeping on Sammy's couch, all to have a late lunch date with a distinguished man with gray hair and a tie in his profile photo who was probably married. But at least she wasn't wearing a push-up bra.

Then her phone rang. An Illinois number. Molly wasn't wearing her blue-tooth headphones but she answered anyway. Maybe someone owed her money.

"Hello?"

"Mom?"

Molly's entire being was sucked into a microscopic dot and then her quarks and leptons built up a mighty electrical charge along with a massive amount of heat and then everything that comprised the universe of Molly exploded outward until she regained her previous shape tucked into the driver seat of her rusted Nissan Altima, fingers tingling on the steering wheel, heart learning how to beat again.

"Are you there?"

"I'm here," Molly said. "I'm here."

"This is Phillip." His pre-pubescent voice lilted with nervousness.

"I knew it was you," Molly said. She wanted to hang up. She wanted to stay on this call forever.

"I need a ride home," he said.

"I'm in Los Angeles."

"Oh. Do you like it there?"

No one ever talked about if they actually liked LA or not. "I don't," she said. "Not really."

"You should move."

"I agree," she said. The car ahead of her inched forward slightly.

"Will you call Dad for me? Tell him I need him to pick me up."

It had been a long time since anyone had required anything from her. "Sure. I can do that."

"Thanks."

Then he hung up.

It was going to take Molly a half an hour to exit and get back on the 405 to return to Sammy's apartment. But there was no way she was going on this lunch date. If the guy in the tie wanted to spend time with her, he'd have to jerk off to her profile picture.

Molly knew what she did to Sammy was wrong. She'd been stringing him along since high school, eager to have someone love her no matter what. A perpetual fan. And when she'd lost her last apartment late last year, she'd convinced Sammy to believe that it was his idea to move to LA and take a higher paying job. And then a few weeks later, she'd asked if she could crash on his brand-new couch.

From afar, Sammy had always been there when she needed him. Sometimes to tell her how beautiful and desirable she was. Sometimes to convince her to keep trying. To keep going on auditions. That she was too talented to fail.

But in the decade since she'd been in LA, she'd needed CODE RED-level help three times:

1) After her first post-marriage break-up from the bass player in Rugged Antlers.
2) When a routine pap smear became a cancer scare.
3) Upon being passed over for the starring role in a CBS sitcom that never aired.

Each time he'd flown out to rescue her. And each time she"d slept with him.

Now Sammy lived here. Anxious for their relationship to move forward. Even though Molly loved him, and she really did love him, she knew they could never be what Sammy imagined. Even if she did leave the couch and move into his bed like he'd been asking. She could never ever give him anything close to what he wanted. He'd made her into a fantasy. The person she was in his head was not the person she was in real life and if Sammy spent any extra time with her, he'd figure it out.

Molly parked her car in Sammy's only covered spot. He'd graciously offered it to her on the first day she'd moved in. She'd graciously accepted. Sammy now parked on the street, which was a bitch, Molly had to confess. Some days it seemed like all of LA was parked on their street.

She climbed the cement stairs to the apartment, Phillip's voice still echoing in her head. Someone out there needed her. It was too overwhelming to comprehend.

The sun reflected on the pool in the middle of the apartment complex. No one was swimming. The whole place felt hazy and indistinct. There wasn't a single sound coming from any of the other apartments.

She opened door 316 and Sammy scrambled out of the kitchen, fumbling something in his hands.

"You're back already?"

"Something incredible happened," Molly said.

Then Sammy got down on one knee and held out an open ring box. His scraggly blond hair was tied behind him, but he was copiously sweating. It was almost audible as it escaped through his pores.

"What the fuck?" Molly said.

"Don't do online dating anymore," Sammy said, his voice hoarse as if he'd been practicing for hours. He had shaved.

"Fine. I'll stop. You don't have to marry me to prove a point." Molly's hands were shaking.

Sammy swayed on his knee. "I'm not proving a point. I'm proving my commitment, Molly."

"Get up, Sammy. Let's talk about this."

Sammy thrust the ring toward her. "Fuck, Molly. I have a good job. Marry me. I don't care if you work."

Molly couldn't look at the ring. She didn't want to see if it was big. If she liked it. If she thought it would look good on her. It was the symbol of the life she craved. The one with the freedom and relaxation she deserved.

"I'm leaving," she said.

"What do you mean?"

"I'm going back to Illinois."

Sammy swayed again. "But I just got here."

"You're doing great. This was an amazing move for you."

"I only moved here to be closer to you."

Molly snuck a peek at the ring. It was beautiful. Simple band. Enormous diamond. "We aren't going to get any closer, Sammy. This is it. I like us the way we are."

"I'm nothing without you, Molly." Sammy hung his head and the ring box slipped from his fingers.

She squatted next to him and rubbed his back.

"Come on, Sammy. You knew this was a desperate ploy. I go out for a lunch date and you go buy a ring."

"I bought it before I moved out here." Tears collected on the carpet like dew.

"But we've never talked about anything like this."

Sammy sunk down until he was sitting on the ground. "I thought we might. I hoped we might."

"It's a beautiful ring. For real. I totally want it. But I need to do the right thing here. Which, as you know, isn't my strongest suit."

"The right thing is for you to find some stability. I'm not stupid. I know you'll never love me like I love you. But I can provide for you. I can support you. And we've had sex before and it wasn't awful."

There was a warmth there. In Molly's chest and up into her neck. A fondness. She continued rubbing his back.

"I have to leave. Tonight. But I promise to think about it. Okay? I promise."

"I feel stupid," Sammy said.

"You aren't stupid. You're the smartest guy I've ever met. And you know me better than I want to admit. Okay? Now get up. And put that ring away."

She helped him to his feet and he slipped the ring box into his pocket. It was a relief to have it gone.

"What time is your flight?" he asked.

"I don't have one yet. But I'll take what I can get."

"I don't understand."

"Me either," Molly said. "I'm just going with the flow."

She suddenly remembered Phillip's request. To call John. It could wait a few more minutes.

"I'm going to pack," Molly said. "Do you think you could give me a lift to the airport?"

4

The cop stared at John without betraying a single emotion. It was perfectly quiet in the lobby, unlike every cop show that John had seen where dozens of stories would be unfolding in the background. People in cuffs. Phones screaming. Detectives being summoned to offices. But here at the local station, there was only the soft hiss of the air conditioner, the periodic gurgles of a water cooler, and the impassively benign face of this police officer who looked permanently fused to his chair. With the focus on John, he found that even though he was losing his shit on the inside, he could only muster a whisper.

"Maybe a half hour," John said.

"So your son's been missing for a half an hour?" the cop said.

"Yes. Well, that's when I was supposed to pick him up from school."

"Could he have taken the bus home?"

"He's never taken the bus."

"But he could have?"

John faltered. He knew that wasn't right. "Sure, he could have I guess."

"What about catching a ride with a friend?"

"His friend is in seventh grade this year."

The cop waited for more.

"Different schools now," John said.

"What about another friend?"

"He doesn't have any other friends."

"Your son has no friends?"

"Well, I don't know," John said. "I'm sure he does have people he talks to."

"Would those be friends, then? These people he talks to."

This was going terribly. "Yes, of course. They could be his friends."

"And presumably he could have gone home with one of them?"

"Yes. Presumably yes. But I know he didn't."

"How do you know?"

"He's never done it before."

"Children are known for their stability and rational thinking, aren't they?" Still no sign of an emotion.

"Not as a group, no," John said. "But Phillip..."

"Is different. I understand. And I know you must be worried about him."

"I'm desperately worried." John's voice rose above a hoarse whisper.

"Here's the thing," the cop said and patted a stack of papers on his desk. "There are a lot of avenues still open as to where Paul might have gone."

"Phillip."

"I'm Officer Martins."

"No, I mean my son's name is Phillip."

"Phillip could be home right now. Have you gone home yet?"

"No," John said abruptly.

"There is no reason to get curt with me, sir. I'm trying to help you."

"But I don't think you are," John said.

"I gave you three possibilities as to what may have happened to your son after school let out. Now I need you to investigate those as well as any other possibilities you can think of. Even if you think they aren't possible. Right now, anything is possible. And if you walk back in here after 24 hours with no sign of Paul, I will fill out this report here so fast you'll wonder how my hand doesn't cramp."

"Phillip," John said.

John emerged from the police station on wobbly legs to find an elderly woman pushing a walker toward the entrance. He opened the door wide and leaned against it, propping it open with the weight of his regret.

He knew he'd upset Phillip more than he'd initially thought. Phillip was clearly upset about Denise being there the previous night. About the encroachment on their insulated world. John had promised to protect Phillip forever and then he'd invited a stranger into their midst. And now, Phillip was rebelling. He was gone.

"Are you escaping?" the elderly woman asked.

"I wish," John said.

"You run now. If anyone comes after you, I'll slam the door on them." She grinned at him and patted him on the arm as she passed through the door. "It can't be as bad as you look."

"I hope you're right."

She turned. "Run!" she said.

So he did.

It felt good. The pavement reverberating through his feet and up his legs. The wind splashing his cheeks. The sense of leaving things behind.

John stopped at his car and heaved breath after breath, sweat stinging his eyes. How had he lost his job and his son in one day?

His phone vibrated in his pocket and he yanked it out expecting to see Phillip's name. Instead he saw THE HARPY in bright letters.

John let it go to voicemail.

A moment later, his text notification lit up.

PHILLIP NEEDS A RIDE.

Only Molly could make this day worse.

CHAPTER SIX

MENDING THE BONES

1

Beth tried her best to hold her arm tightly against her midsection as Denise apparently aimed for every pothole in the county.

"So, we're out now. How did you break your arm?" Denise asked without looking over.

Of course, it wasn't only her arm that Beth was hugging against her. It was also the hard cast and a dark blue sling. Plus the memory of Renata's distraught face as Beth got to her feet at the bottom of the stairs and assured her she was fine.

"Come on. I told you about Mom," Denise said. "Even though I was sworn to secrecy with threat of removal from her will."

Beth scoffed. "She's not going to take you out."

"I don't care about the will."

"Yes, you do," Beth said. "That's why you almost didn't tell me."

Beth's arm ached, and her ego ached, and she was so hungry she was ready to gnaw off her other arm like James Franco in 127 Hours. And she hadn't even begun dealing with the fact that her mom was dying.

"Not fair," Denise said as the car bounced over another pothole. "I can be devastatingly sad and worried about my inheritance at the same time."

Beth unclenched her jaw. "What are you hoping to get? The house?"

"I don't know, Beth. I'm not expecting anything. I just don't like change. And I can't imagine life without Mom."

Denise looked legitimately distraught.

"She's your main source of income, isn't she?" Beth said.

"You're the one living with her."

"You don't have to get defensive."

"I'm upset. Mom's going to be gone soon. And you suddenly end up in the hospital and won't tell me why."

One thing Fran had always said was that Beth couldn't see things from anyone else's point of view. So Beth tried to imagine the day Denise was having. Finding out Mom was dying. Sworn to secrecy. Worried about how she would support herself going forward.

Beth exhaled loudly so Denise would know how hard her internal struggle had been. "I freaked out, okay? I'm going through a breakup, and I wasn't sure if someone was coming on to me or not."

"A guy broke your arm? This is fucking serious, Beth."

Denise was so dense that it caused new parts of Beth to ache. "You know it wasn't a guy."

"I don't understand."

"Do I really have to come out to you?" Beth said. "Can't we just stick with inference and subterfuge? You don't have to approve."

Denise's clueless expression gave it all away.

"You don't know? How could you not know?"

Ones and zeroes began to whir now, and Beth could see Denise processing them like a computer from the 80s. Unearthing hints from their childhood. Like maybe the fact Beth had never had a boyfriend. Or more overtly, the way Beth used to make out with girls in her bedroom during sleepovers. Or even more overtly, all the k.d. lang CDs.

"Oh," Denise said.

"So it wasn't some big beefy biker dude or whatever you conjured from the chasm that separates us. It was a girl I used to know who can't possible weigh more than 100 pounds. And I fell down the stairs. In Mom's house."

Denise continued to drive but the road was suddenly smooth. Nothing could dislodge this awkward conversation.

"I thought everyone knew," Beth said.

"How can I know if you never told me?"

"People know stuff about each other. I don't know. We're closer now."

"Does Taylor know?"

Beth shrugged and then winced. "I'm the wrong person to ask. Like I said, I thought you knew."

The car bumped as Denise steered toward a gas station where she parked in front of the window of a rundown convenience store.

"It's not a big deal that you're gay," Denise said. "I'm just upset at the reminders that we grew so far apart. That we're still far apart. Why did we all do that? All three of us?"

Beth knew exactly why they had dispersed one by one after Dad died. It was Mom. She hadn't been strong enough to hold them together. Dad was her everything. And the three of them combined weren't even close. They were nothing compared to him. Instead of them grieving together, Mom had turned her sadness into disappointment and it drove each of them away. It was as if Mom had waited for one of her children to step up and be her everything, and when they couldn't, she'd held it against them.

"White people," Beth finally said. "We're white people. We grow apart. And we don't look out for each other."

Denise nodded. "I mean, doesn't Mom know she's supposed to wait around until we can put her in an old folk's home?"

"Exactly. She's not getting the full package."

"Are we being funny?"

"No," Beth said. "Not at all."

"Should we go into this convenience store and ransack the snack section?"

"I can't think of single thing I'd rather do."

Denise gave her a serious look. "Follow my lead."

The cashier glanced up from a magazine he was careful to keep covered. Cartons of cigarettes loomed behind him.

"He won't notice," Denise said.

Beth followed her past a metal rack filled with dishwashing detergent, potato chips, and tiny keychain flashlights toward a dusty candy aisle.

"Pick what you want and hand it to me."

Beth scanned the shelf and settled on two Three Musketeer bars, three Kit Kats, and a package of Starburst. She handed them to Denise who was already cradling quite a haul of Twizzlers and Reese's peanut butter cups in her folded arms.

Then she disappeared.

A thrill pulsed through Beth's veins. It had been so long since she'd seen her sister use her gift. So long in fact, that it had been easy for her to pretend it wasn't real. Then there was the secondary thrill of being in the convenience store and knowing that Denise was going to walk out without paying. That she'd done it before. That she'd do it again.

"Now just go. I'll be right behind you." Denise's voice was closer than Beth expected.

But Beth remained there, letting the moment be a moment. She wanted to remember the smell of the shop. That mix of sweat and exhaust and Cool Ranch Doritos. She wanted to remember the way the light glinted off the handle of the ice cream freezer like diamonds. The way her feet stuck slightly to the floor. The way the vent above her rattled like a loose cough. She needed to remember the precise second that she was saved.

"Stop grinning like a fool. You're going to give us away."

"Follow me," Beth said as she walked toward the front of the store.

The cashier looked up, expectantly.

"Not today," Beth said and opened the door. She felt Denise rush past her, packaging ruffling slightly. Beth had forgotten that whatever Denise was holding would disappear with her. The possibilities were endless for what the two of them could accomplish going forward. Life suddenly looked exciting again.

Beth ran around to the passenger side of the car, her cheeks sore from grinning. She wasn't made to be happy. She didn't have the stamina.

She sat down and stretched across the center console, reaching to open the door for Denise who must be standing on the outside. A large black van had parked next to them and its passenger door suddenly flung open. There was a soft sound, like someone punching a bag of flour, and Denise lurched back into view as she fell hard to the pavement, chocolate and candy spraying up into the air between the two vehicles.

"Oh shit," a man with a massive black beard said. "I didn't see you there."

Through the driver's window, Beth watched him lean down and help Denise to her feet.

There was blood.

Beth drove now, her broken left arm tucked on her lap. Denise sat in the passenger seat, tears running down her cheeks as she peered at herself in the vanity mirror. Beth couldn't look for long because it sent sympathy pain into her own cheeks. The right side of Denise's face, specifically under her eye, was already turning black and her top lip was split open like a hotdog cooked too long. But her nose. Oh god, her nose.

"I think it's broken," Beth said.

"Just don't crash my car," Denise said as if her sinuses were stuffed with cotton.

Beth could guess how she felt. After she had landed with a somewhat graceful thud at the foot of the stairs, she hadn't known her arm was broken. Her first instinct had been to laugh.

"Stuck the landing," she had said.

"I think your arm's broken," Renata had said.

Then they'd driven in silence to the hospital and that was when the pain had settled in. Now that she and Denise were a few minutes past the accident, she knew Denise's face must hurt something fierce.

"You want to unwrap a Kit Kat for me?" Beth said.

"My nose is bleeding."

"You could lean back a little."

Denise started opening one. "So I get clobbered by a car door, splayed on the ground, and you take a moment to pick up snacks."

"You weren't on the ground anymore. We'd already gotten you into the car. Before I got in to drive, I picked up whatever the two of you hadn't stepped on."

"Oh, sorry. How inconsiderate of me."

"Apology accepted."

Denise threw the Kit Kat at her, but Beth managed to catch it in her lap.

"How bad do I look?" Denise asked as she turned her attention back to the mirror.

"Are you expecting me to bend reality?" Beth said. "You look terrible, which I know you can see."

Denise touched her nose and winced. "Do you believe in karma?"

Beth laughed loudly, her belly banging against her aching arm. "Never in a million years."

"Total horseshit," Denise said.

Beth laughed even louder. She steered them toward the emergency room, an explosion of sunset in the sky behind the hospital. "We're back," she said.

2

Phillip sat at Mrs. Clark's dining table with a glass of chocolate milk and a twisty straw, and it didn't feel like a kidnapping. Todd Crandell would be disappointed. He'd probably wanted Phillip to disappear forever too, so he could scare another kid with the story.

Mrs. Clark sat down across from him. She also had a glass of chocolate milk with a twisty straw. Phillip watched as the chocolate milk pirouetted through the straw, finally arriving at her chapped lips. She made a really long 'mmmmm' sound.

"I stocked the fridge with this when my daughter Denise stayed for a week last month. It was her favorite when she was a kid, but apparently, it's not her favorite anymore."

"Chocolate milk is great," Phillip said.

"Exactly what I said, but she's too good for it now. I'm glad you're here to appreciate it."

Phillip took a long sip.

Mrs. Clark sighed. "But you didn't come here for a drink. Tell me what you were doing in my car. What is this investigation?"

"It's nothing," Phillip said.

"Wait a minute," she said, getting excited. "This is the kidnapping story again, isn't it? It's been a while. You must have heard it from Todd Crandell. I see you two spending time together. I had his older brother years ago."

"I'm sorry," Phillip said as his straw tapped against the side of his glass.

"You don't have to apologize. I probably would have done the same thing if I heard such a fantastic story. You want to solve the mystery?"

Mrs. Clark stared at him with a weird glint in her eye that kind of scared Phillip. Maybe she was planning to keep him after all.

"There was a boy, long before Todd's brother. His parents were moving in the middle of the year. I think divorce but I can't remember now. Anyway, on his last day of school, he hid in my car. Just like you. Except I noticed right away because I wasn't old and doddering yet. I offered to drive him home but first we got ice cream and I told him how meaningless his move would feel in a few years. Even in a few weeks. And that was that. But he never came to school again. And the last place he was seen was in my car."

Her story made perfect sense. But Phillip felt uneasy with her staring at him. Luckily, she closed her eyes and took another pull on the straw.

"So, do you believe me?" she said after smacking her lips loudly.

"I don't know."

"Want to look around? See if you see any signs of malfeasance?"

She was laughing at him now even though he could guess what malfeasance meant. It meant bad stuff. He still hadn't decided if there was bad stuff going on. He sort of did want to look around.

"You're considering it, aren't you?" She looked pleased. "Can't take someone at their word. If you're going to investigate, you have to search for the truth on your own."

Phillip hoped his dad would be here as soon as possible. He wondered if his mom had called him. He still felt numb after hearing her voice. As if she'd pulled part of him through the phone to Los Angeles and what remained was sort of ghostly or at least a little see-through. Maybe Mrs. Clark was staring so much because she could see inside of him. His heart pumping fast behind his ribs. His bladder like a water balloon. His fear glowing in his veins like the gold those people went looking for in rivers during the Gold Rush.

"Have you read Agatha Christie? Or Sir Arthur Conan Doyle?"

"I don't think so," Phillip said.

"Oh, Phillip. I'm going to blow your mind."

Mrs. Clark got up with a grunt and moved into the next room. There was a massive dining table that didn't look like it got much use. On the far wall was a bookshelf that was so full of books, it seemed impossible it was still standing. She knelt in front of it and pulled a thick volume from the middle shelf. "Every Sherlock Holmes story."

She blew some dust from the cover and then she tipped over in slow motion. Her back slammed against the bookshelf and then she thumped to the floor. All of her muscles tensed at once and she began to vibrate like an egg in boiling water.

"Mrs. Clark?"

There was a whimpering noise coming out of her now, like the dog next door when he couldn't get back into the house.

Phillip backed away. She tapped the book she'd picked for him with the tip of her shoe. He didn't want to leave her, but he was overwhelmed by an urge to wait for his dad outside. What if his dad didn't know the correct house? What if he was driving up and down the street right now looking for him? What if all it would take would be to see Phillip sitting outside?

He looked away from Mrs. Clark and walked through the kitchen and out the front door. A wind sputtered as he sat on the cement step, his feet resting on the small sidewalk that followed the side of the garage around to the driveway. He breathed in and out and in and out and in and out until the door opened behind him.

Mrs. Clark sat on the step next to him. "Whoops," she said.

Phillip knew he should say something, but all the words were in the wrong order.

"Well, I might as well tell you. I'm dying, Phillip. Very soon."

Phillip squeezed his eyes shut and leaned forward over his knees. "Are you scared?"

"I think so," she said and then took a deep breath. "Quite a bit actually."

"Why?"

"I like existing. I like being me."

"I like you too, Mrs. Clark."

"Thanks, Phillip. That means a whole lot to me. It really does. More than you know."

"So that's why you were acting so weird? Because you're... you know." Phillip hugged his knees to his chest and then looked over at her.

"Yes, it's not because I once kidnapped another boy and decided to strike again." She smiled and then frowned.

"That's good."

"Hey, we can't be mooning around when your dad shows up."

"Okay," Phillip said.

She suddenly began laughing maniacally. She nudged him.

"Come on. Start laughing."

He tried but it came out like he was gargling mouthwash.

"You can do better than that! Like this. From the gut." She put her hand on her stomach and leaned her head back and started bellowing. But there was an edge there now. Like maybe it wasn't all fake. Maybe she was really laughing.

Phillip put his hand on his stomach and leaned back his head too. And this time the laugh came out like a laugh.

"Keep going!" Mrs. Clark said.

He laughed some more and then something changed in his chest.

"I'm really laughing now," he said.

"Me too, Phillip. Me too."

3

John was angry. Like unable to stop shaking angry. Phillip disappears from school and when he needs help he calls Molly? John spent years wiping his ass and buying him clothes and getting him prepared for school and then doing homework with him and consoling him when he needed it and cheering him when he needed it more and cooking so much food and staying up late to read recipes to make his favorite foods and more than once explaining what a boner was and worrying about him all the time and loving him like it was a job and loving him like it was a compulsion and finally just loving him and cooking so much more food and jettisoning any semblance of the life he had before. How the fuck did he even know Molly's number?

Then John had to call Phillip's teacher and look like a total asshole: Yeah, I don't know where my kid is, but my ex-wife in Los Angeles who has never spoken to him knows exactly where he is. Cool.

Now Phillip's recently unemployed dad whose piece of shit Dodge with the doors that screeched like a raccoon caught in a trap and a bungee cord holding the hood in place was sputtering across town belching out carbon monoxide, was replaying the one-and-a-half minute conversation he'd had with the ex-wife who had disappeared one afternoon and left him with a six-month old son and wondering if she still looked as good as she used to and hating himself more than he had ever hated himself in his entire life.

Then when he turned onto the teacher's street there they were, his son and his teacher, laughing huge belly laughs on the porch and he knew they were laughing at him. Phillip was parsing his failures, relaying his ineptitude, and just spinning a good old yarn about his miserable excuse of a dad. And look how they laughed! John's brand of incompetence only came around once a generation. It had to be observed and ridiculed to be truly savored.

So John drove past. Abandoned him. Let them have their laugh. They could laugh all night for all he cared. Then John got two streets away and did a U-turn and went straight back. They were still laughing so he drove past again. He pulled over a block away and breathed. He knew Molly was still beautiful.

Who was he kidding? He should have told Brad Green to go fuck himself. That much was obvious. And after he'd gotten fired, he should have taken Phillip out of school early and gone to that place he wanted to go with all-you-can-eat soft serve. What kind of moron was he? He should have gotten Denise's phone number. Or even a last name. Some way to reach her again. His regret sucked all the air out of the car, and he rolled down the window. It screeched even louder than the door and startled a woman walking her dog.

"I'm poor," John said. "I don't live in this neighborhood."

"Should I call the cops?" the woman asked, while her dog made little huffing noises.

"I'm just picking up my son. I thought he was missing earlier, and I tried to file a report at the police station, but they wouldn't let me. Turns out he has to be gone for at least 24 hours. You know how much can happen in 24 hours?"

The woman stayed on the sidewalk across the street, but she turned to face him. She was older than he'd thought. Maybe in her fifties. "I'm pretty sure I knew that," she said. "I think I heard it in a movie. You found him?"

"Yes, he's one street over. But he's out front laughing with his teacher and I felt stupid, so I pulled over here."

"Well at least you found him. I hope you have a better night." She whistled at her dog and they continued on their way. At the corner, her dog took a massive shit, and John watched her pick it up with a small bag. When she was out of sight, he drove back up the block and pulled into Phillip's teacher's driveway.

They weren't laughing anymore. They were just sitting in silence. John opened the door as slowly as possible hoping to make the least amount of noise.

"I'm sorry about this, Mrs. Clark," John said, his hands up in a weird defensive gesture as he moved up the walkway. Like he expected her to hurl herself at him and claw out his eyes. "I don't know what came over Phillip. I promise it won't happen again."

"I'm sure that it won't," she said as she got to her feet. "But it was perfectly fine."

John hadn't really looked at Phillip and he was pretty sure Phillip hadn't looked at him. But then suddenly Phillip was walking toward him. He had his head down and after a few shuffling steps, he was pressed against John, his arms wrapped tightly around him.

"It's okay, buddy," John said. He rubbed Phillip's hair.

"He's had a strange day," Mrs. Clark said. "But I hope you'll forgive him. I feel like no punishment is needed. I'm actually glad he stopped by."

"It's okay, right, Dad?" Phillip said with his face pressed against John's chest.

"Of course. You still want to go out to dinner?" John knew it might be the last time for a long time. Whatever small amount of money was still owed to him from the law firm would be gone in a matter of weeks.

"I just want to go home," Phillip said. "If that's okay with you."

"Yes, absolutely. But we can't do anything with you clutching me like I'm going to float away." He tried a smile and it almost worked.

Phillip pulled away, his head still down. He walked around to the passenger side and got in.

"Well, I'm glad he wasn't a nuisance," John said to Mrs. Clark.

"You have a wonderful boy there," she said.

"I do indeed."

A car pulled along the curb and John watched as two women got out. One had her arm in a sling and the other had a white medical tape across the bridge of her nose and horrific black eye.

Inexplicably, the one with the black eye was Denise.

John's heart beat one massive burst and all of his blood rocketed out to his extremities. It was like a firecracker going off inside him.

"John?" she said.

He remembered the way she'd felt next to him as he had drifted off to sleep last night. The last good thing that had happened.

"Can I get your phone number?" he said.

4

A plane departed Los Angeles with Molly on board. She said no to peanuts but yes to a ginger ale.

CHAPTER SEVEN

MITIGATING THE EMOTIONS

1

Something had changed. It was that moment after they'd finished laughing. The silence overwhelming in its immensity. It was the silence that preceded the Big Bang. It was the silence at the lowest point of the ocean. It was the silence of death. Beginnings and endings are always devoid of sound. Mute. Impotent. Solitary.

"You're just like my dad," Phillip had said.

"What do you mean?" Edna had pushed the words up from her lungs where they'd ricocheted off lymph nodes and tonsils and her tongue and two rows of teeth until they barely registered as a sound.

"Lonely," he'd said.

Oh Nolan, you asshole. Why did you leave so early?

"It was the only way to get away from you," the glioblastoma heckled.

"Go away," Edna said. "You don't scare me."

Then Beth's expansive face was directly in front of her, warped at the edges, filling every available viewing space.

"Mom?"

Edna stepped away to find herself standing in her driveway, the sky purpled with oncoming night. Phillip was gone. In his place were Denise and Beth looking as if they'd barely survived a cage match.

"Are you alright?" Beth said with way too much concern.

"Me?" Edna said. "Your arm is broken. And Denise's face is taped together."

"Long story," Denise said.

"Well, tell me later. I'd like to go inside."

Her two daughters moved forward and each grabbed one of her elbows as if she were going to topple to the ground at any moment. Of course, Denise had told Beth about her impending death. Why wouldn't she? Taking care of her dying mom would give Denise the purpose she craved.

"If I fall, I promise I'll let you pick me up," Edna said. "But until then, let's see what happens."

They let go and followed her to the house.

When Edna got to the door she stopped and turned toward them. Her bedraggled and disheveled daughters. Denise's face looked truly painful. Something had happened today to beat her two girls down. But maybe, just maybe, they would fight back. Edna wasn't going to be here much longer to bail them out.

"I want to set some rules," Edna said.

They both nodded.

"We don't talk about it. And by "it" you know exactly what I mean, so don't try to be coy. Come in. We can eat something. Well, maybe not you, Denise. I don't know how you could open your mouth wide enough."

"Thanks, Mom," Denise said.

"I have twisty straws," Edna said, and Beth laughed.

"That's a relief," Denise said.

Edna continued staring at them. "I'm serious. We go in. We eat. You tell me what happened to you. No sad faces. No feeling sorry for me. A normal night."

"You got it, Mom," Beth said.

"And Denise," Edna said. "You're out of my will."

"Dammit," Denise said. She had no idea if her mom was serious.

2

Phillip looked out his window and saw Suz's mailbox hanging open like a gasping fish. That was the sign for him to come around back and knock on her window as soon as he could. She hadn't used it much since she'd gone off to middle school, but Phillip took it very seriously.

His dad was sitting on the couch in the front room staring at the television. But it was off. He was staring at the reflection of himself, still in his work shirt and pants, shaking his left knee up and down so vigorously that his cheeks were vibrating.

"Change your mind?" his dad asked.

"About what?" Phillip said, his eye on the front door.

"Dinner. I'd love to still take you to dinner."

"Actually, I was going to run over to Suz for a minute. I need to tell her something."

His dad shook his head, and Phillip felt an infinite sadness for him.

"Can we go tomorrow?" Phillip suggested.

"Of course. I'd like that. Don't stay out long. You have school tomorrow."

"I won't," Phillip said, and practically ran out the door. He stopped briefly in the grass, trying to pinpoint the precise spot the invisible woman had stood, then he crossed the street and hopped the fence into Suz's backyard.

Her light was on, but her blinds were closed. Phillip knocked lightly.

Within seconds, Suz peered through the slats.

"Look who finally showed up."

"It's been a long day," Phillip said.

"What happened to our dinner?"

"Sorry, I can explain. Are you coming out?"

The blinds snapped closed again and the light went out.

Phillip returned to the front curb to wait for her. He wondered if the invisible woman would come back. Maybe she was there right now. How had she known that he and his dad would be at Mrs. Clark's house? What had happened to her face? This was even better than the Mrs. Clark kidnapping mystery. They were all tied together somehow, and Phillip wanted to figure it out. He wished that Mrs. Clark had remembered to give him that mystery book. There were probably a lot of pointers about solving mysteries in there. He hoped she'd bring it to school tomorrow.

Suz joined him on the curb.

"They're fighting again," she said. "All the usual threats of divorce sprinkled with some of death."

"Murder or suicide?" Phillip asked.

"Both."

"I'm sorry, Suz. They'll make up."

"I wish they'd stop. They think they're making up for me. If they bothered to ask what I actually wanted, I'd tell them to get divorced already. Get on with their lives. But I don't think they'd even hear me. It's like they're screaming at each other through opposite ends of a garden hose."

"You wrote that line in your journal, didn't you?" Phillip said.

Suz smiled. "Right before you showed up."

"I can picture it. The garden hose. Their angry faces."

"You want to go somewhere with me?"

Phillip glanced at his house. Silent. He didn't want to return just yet.

"Sure. Where are we going?"

"I need a cigarette."

Phillip followed Suz down McLean Avenue, cars hissing across the asphalt behind them. Colors were swallowed by a canopy of gloom. Phillip let Suz walk two steps ahead of him, her tennis shoes slapping on the sidewalk. Fuh-lup, fuh-lup. Other than a quick look back as she cut across a field, it was like she had forgotten he was there. Until they got to the construction site. She leaped over a tilted fence like she'd been there dozens of times. Phillip was worried about entering private property, but he would never say that to Suz.

Steel beams pointed toward the sky; a roof crisscrossed above them. They stepped onto the cement floor and left muddy footprints behind them. The shape of the building had only recently become clear; a small L-shaped gas station. Suz walked to the back and waved her arms. "I bet there's a refrigerator full of beer here," she said, her voice echoing slightly above them. "The cashier will probably know my dad's name."

Phillip could see Suz's dad here, a six-pack in each hand. "Cash register will be over there," he said and gestured across the cement.

"My dad will get all his porn here for sure." She hunched her shoulders and lowered her voice: "Got the new issue of Juggs?"

"That doesn't sound like your dad at all." Phillip wondered if his dad bought his magazines at a gas station. "Don't forget the Slurpee machine," he said.

"Oh right, that'll be back there." She looked back to where they had entered. "We just walked through it, like a couple of ghosts."

Phillip pointed into the corner above them. "They'll have a camera there."

"Of course. So they can catch our dads buying those magazines."

"In the middle here, they'll have shelves for candy."

"And potato chips."

Suz stopped abruptly, her lips slightly parted, her hands balled in front of her. "I held someone's hand today."

"Oh." The chasm between them grew every day. Phillip's hand ached with a desire to know what Suz's hand felt like.

"Are you upset?" she asked.

"I think I might be."

Suz bowed her head. "I thought about you. I wondered."

"I'm pretty sure Todd Crandell wants to hold your hand too," Phillip said.

"He definitely does," Suz said. "Not going to happen."

The sense of relief shocked him with its intensity. "You think this guy is going to hold your hand again?"

"Only if I say it's okay," Suz said.

"Is it okay?"

She narrowed her eyes at him. "I don't know yet."

"What's his name?"

"Jordan."

Phillip tried to picture what a Jordan would look like. It wasn't good.

Suz tried to shrug off the conversation. "Anyway. It seemed important so I wanted to tell you."

"I'm glad you did." Phillip swallowed. "I want to tell you something important too."

Suz tugged his arm, and he followed her through the beams to a cement island where the gas pumps would surely be installed. She sat down heavily and patted the spot next to her. Phillip glanced out toward the road, convinced that a cop would come and arrest them for trespassing at any moment.

"We aren't going to get in trouble," she said. "I come here all the time."

"You never told me that."

"Sometimes I just want to be alone."

Phillip nodded and sat next to her.

"What is the important thing you wanted to tell me?" she said.

He suddenly felt silly. He barely believed himself about an invisible woman anymore. And he wasn't sure if this new, older version of Suz would understand.

"I talked to my mom," he said.

"Was it everything you hoped?"

"Not really. She was just a voice. Just some lady. I didn't feel anything."

"She did you a favor, you know? She ran off before she and your dad could turn into my parents."

Phillip sniffled. "I don't know. I wish I knew her."

"It's overrated. Knowing your mom." Suz reached into her pocket and pulled out a purple lighter. "Have you ever smoked a cigarette?"

"No."

"Well, it's not hard at all. Help me find a few."

She jumped to her feet and began dragging her shoes across the gravel. She stooped and picked up a half-smoked butt. She looked at Phillip. "What are you waiting for?"

"Those have already been in someone's mouth."

"Unless you know a place that's going to sell them to us."

Phillip pictured a man with stubble and decaying teeth, his chapped lips working their way around the cigarette. The man pulled it from his mouth with dirty hands and spit onto the gravel. There was no way that Phillip was putting one of them in his mouth.

"Are you going to let me down?"

Phillip stood and scanned the cigarette butts scattered across the gravel.

"Try to find the ones that aren't too flat," Suz said as she knelt again.

They returned to the concrete island a few minutes later. Phillip gingerly palmed two butts while Suz held a small mountain. "That's pathetic." She laughed.

They put them in a pile between them and Suz flicked the lighter a few times. "These are only good for a few puffs, if that," she said. "So it's best if you have it in your mouth when you light it."

Phillip narrowed his eyes and leaned away from her.

"Fine, I'll show you." She grabbed one of the plumper specimens and placed it delicately on her lips. She brought the lighter to the tip and gave it a flick. A flame hurled from the plastic casing and charred the end of the cigarette. Suz inhaled immediately and the butt glowed a bright orange.

It burned down to her fingers, and she quickly threw it to the side, her cheeks swelled out like a chipmunk. Phillip watched her, the whites of her eyes widening. Then she let out a cloud of smoke, tears running down her cheeks. She hacked loudly and Phillip wanted to put his hand on her back more than he'd ever wanted to do anything in his life.

Suz doubled over her legs and coughed loudly between her knees. She took a few deep breaths and then righted herself. "That was a good one."

"I thought you were going to throw up," Phillip said.

"Only the first time." She picked up another a cigarette and held it out to him. "Your turn."

"I don't know," he said.

"Never mind. You don't have to smoke a cigarette," she said. "I'm sorry I dragged you out here."

"I want to."

"No, you don't. You think it's gross."

Phillip pursed his lips. "It's not like we know where they've been."

Suz studied the cigarette in her hand, spinning it slightly, lifting and lowering it to look at all angles. Then she put it in her mouth and held it there, air escaping from her nose in bursts. When she was done, she slowly removed it from her lips and held it out to him again. "Now you know where it's been."

Phillip suddenly wanted to tell her about the invisible woman. How he knew it sounded crazy, but it was true. She could disappear. And how he'd seen her again with bandages on her face. In a rush, Phillip realized he hadn't even told Suz about his ride in the back of Mrs. Clark's car. How she convulsed on the floor. About how she was dying. And how devastating that was to know.

But he didn't say anything. Instead, he picked up the cigarette and put it in his mouth.

It tasted like straw, or at least how he figured straw must taste. Musty and stale. He tried to roll it, but it had stuck to his lips. Not even a full minute ago it had been in Suz's mouth and he felt a ripple of warmth run across his neck.

"You alright?" she asked.

"Yes."

She put the lighter down next to him. "You know how to use that?"

"Yes." He'd seen enough people on TV and movies to figure it out. He just had to rub his thumb along the back.

"Take your time."

He picked up the lighter and held it out in front of him. He turned the knob on the back but only produced a scraping sound.

"You have to do it faster," Suz said. "Like you're trying to break it."

Phillip pulled his thumb back and a flame shot up only to rescind in the same instant.

"Well, then you have to hold that button down. On the back."

Phillip tried again and this time, the flame danced in front of him. He instinctively pushed his lips out, getting the cigarette as far away from his face. He delicately put the flame to the end.

"Inhale, Phillip. Inhale!"

He sucked in a mouthful of rancid air that burned the back of his throat the moment it entered. The cigarette fell from his lips and danced on the gravel between his feet. His esophagus constricted and his body forced his mouth open.

Smoke poured out of his mouth and nose, flooding his eyes. His ears rang. His tongue swelled. The gas station spun in front of him like a kaleidoscope.

"Breathe," Suz said softly and patted him on the back.

He released his breath and began coughing uncontrollably. Bile swirled in his chest. He didn't want to throw up in front of Suz. He leaned over and stared at his shoes, the ends of the laces frayed, the soles detached in the back. He let out a few more hacks and then finally took a breath that didn't send him into spasms. He sat up and ran his arm across his eyes; suddenly aware of how close Suz was to him and how intently she was staring at him.

"I guess I needed a cigarette too," he said.

She handed him another one.

3

Beth sat in her room with her DVDs and posters and the same sheets from high school and she felt sorry for herself. Her arm ached. She wanted Fran to call. She wanted Renata to call. She wanted to break through the window and fly into the sky. But she felt too heavy. There was her laptop, open on her unmade bed. There was the stack of candy she'd gotten with Denise. There was Beth lying on her back, a pillow propped under the elbow of her broken arm. There was one single dried tear streak on Beth's cheek. Deep inside, there was an ache. Inside that ache, there was regret. Inside that regret was shame. Beth was never going to get up again.

Then her phone rang, and she had to disrupt her pitiable tableau.

She lifted herself from the bed, wincing as her arm bumped against her side. She closed her laptop and slid to the end of the bed, placing both of her feet on the floor, before answering her phone.

"What?"

"We have to tell Taylor," Denise said on the other line.

"You're already out of the will so I'll leave it to you," Beth said. She leaned down and began painfully putting on her shoes.

"I can't reach him."

"No surprise there."

"You need to stop lying in bed and feeling sorry for yourself."

"You don't know what I'm doing."

"Of course, I do. Now get dressed and meet me downstairs."

"No."

Denise sighed. "I'm sitting in the driveway."

"Thanks for the update."

"We're going to drive into the city and find Taylor."

"No."

"Just get down here."

"No," Beth said again. But she was already walking down the stairs.

CHAPTER EIGHT

EMBRACING THE BAD IDEAS

1

Maybe the old joke went like this: a paraplegic man rolled into a bar. Because that's exactly what happened. Except the guy in the wheelchair wasn't a stranger. Taylor had been laying down tracks in the man's recording studio for the last week. Gill's low ends were notorious, and Taylor had saved for two years to afford time in his studio. The result was the best stuff he'd ever done. Like the fucking Flaming Lips swallowed Fugazi and spit up the resulting mush for The Shins to consume and then they aged ten years and got their 10,000 hours.

The next step was for Taylor to write the press material that no one would read. No manager would help him get reviewed at Pitchfork, and no bookers would give him a prime opening spot for a touring national band. Of course, these new songs would never break the 'one thousand listens' barrier on Spotify and then the band he'd assembled to play these songs live would slowly dissipate. And then he'd start thinking about all that money he'd spent.

But in the studio, with Gill next to him, a guy who seemed to believe in these songs as much as Taylor, he'd felt like a real recording musician for the first time. And that's why they'd spent so much time putting the songs together that Taylor was out of money. He'd booked more and more time that he couldn't afford, desperate to have this finished five song EP. The band was stoked. There was magic every time they recorded. They had finished tracking and were now mixing. Hours and hours of tweaking small knobs to nudge sounds that Taylor couldn't hear. But Gill was the expert. He trusted Gill with everything. With the future of his music.

Once the money had run out, Taylor had offered a deal. Something he hadn't done in years. In lieu of payment, Taylor had been healing Gill. And now Gill had shown up at the bar only one session before he was going to hand over the final mixes. Before he hooked Taylor up with his contacts in LA. Before he helped him find a couch to crash on if he decided to move there. Before their time together came to an end.

"You weren't lying," Gill said, his craggy face attempting a smile. His voice sounded like he was plugged into a distortion pedal.

"What do you mean?" Taylor said.

"That you spend every night in this bar."

"Well, it's less than a block from my apartment."

"This is a shitty neighborhood," a woman said from behind Gill. Taylor hadn't realized they'd been together. She was tall with a long face and tight curly black hair.

Taylor leaned onto the bar, his right elbow sticking on some sweet drink that the lady next to him had been sipping a half hour ago. She'd turned him down before he'd even finished his pick-up line.

Marcus limped over while wiping an empty glass, like a cliché of every bartender in every music video ever. Bald on top, party in the back.

"The lady says this is a shitty neighborhood," Taylor said.

Marcus snorted. "I'll charge you double for drinks so you feel like you're somewhere ritzier."

"I'm not drinking," she said.

"Hope that means you're buying," Taylor said.

"This is Kacie," Gill said from his chair. "The one I was telling you about."

Gill had never mentioned her once during their weeks of recording.

"Charmed," Taylor said.

"He certainly told me about you," Kacie said. "And that nonsense you packed into his head."

"It's not nonsense." Gill leaned forward and his wheelchair creaked underneath him. "I want to show her," he said as his bulbous eyes strained at their sockets.

Taylor could feel his magnificent EP slipping away. He'd known healing him was a bad idea from the start, but he'd wanted to complete this project. He wanted to finally have something he was proud to share. But when he healed people, it wasn't permanent. Now Gill had had a taste of something he'd been living without for years. No matter what Taylor did in this moment, by the end of the night, Gill would hate him. Which would be the best-case scenario. Taylor had to live daily with the consequences of a worst-case scenario.

"We had a deal," Taylor said.

"I'll give you more recording time."

"But we're done," Taylor said. "You said one more session. Some last tweaks and then off to mastering."

"I played them for Kacie. She liked them, didn't you?"

Kacie shrugged. "I've heard worse."

"We could do a few more," Gill said.

"Go home, Gill," Taylor said. "I'll see you at the studio tomorrow."

Gill's grip on his arm was much tighter than Taylor expected. "I'm not going home until we show Kacie." Saliva collected in the corners of his tightened mouth.

"Yeah," Kacie said, her expression like a middle finger. "Show me."

"I'm sorry, I can't," Taylor said.

"Total bullshit," Kacie said. "I can't believe you dragged me out for this loser."

Gill began pulling Taylor's arm toward him. "Show her."

Taylor yanked his arm away as Marcus banged the empty glass onto the bar. "Maybe you two should go," he growled.

"Good idea," Kacie said.

"Come on, Taylor," Gill pleaded. "I need this."

"I want the finished tracks tonight."

"You got it," Gill said. "Anything."

"Right after. We go get them. Promise me."

"I promise," Gill said.

Taylor looked around the bar. This would be the last time he was here. He'd miss Marcus. He'd have to ditch that shit apartment too. Go somewhere Gill couldn't track him down. Guess he'd have to regroup at his mom's house again. Just like last time.

"Two things," Taylor said.

"Anything," Gill said.

"Promise me you won't commit suicide."

"You don't have to listen to this shit," Kacie said.

Gill held up his hand like he was on trial for stealing a song. "I promise. What's the other thing?"

"Buy me another drink."

Kacie stepped toward the bar. "One watered down beer for my new friend here." She looked down at Taylor's hands. "What's with the gloves?"

Taylor rubbed his hands together, both encased in thin black gloves made from the softest rabbit fur he could find. The gloves didn't stop the effect, but they dulled it a bit. He only took them off when he was playing music. Or convincing Gill to give him more studio time.

Marcus poured Taylor a beer. "You okay here?"

"It's fine, Marcus. I'll be fine."

Kacie banged a few bills on the bar. "Now what, Mr. Magic Man?"

"Not in here. You have a car?"

"I have a car and a job," Kacie said. "What about you?"

In response, Taylor picked up the beer and drank half of it.

"Save that for me," Taylor said to Marcus and got to his feet. Only slightly unsteady.

"I'll have to charge a storage fee," Marcus said with a laugh.

Taylor pointed at Kacie. "She's good for it."

Kacie slapped another bill on the table.

"After you," Taylor said.

Gill spun his chair toward the door, and Taylor had to double step it to keep up. The dude could move.

Outside was humid, the air crackling with the possibility of rain. Glass popped under the wheels of Gill's chair. The susurration of cars on the highway crescendoed and decrescendoed around them.

Kacie opened the passenger door of a gleaming blue Toyota, and Gill hoisted himself inside. With a practiced ease, Kacie folded his chair and tossed it into the trunk.

"Can we forget about this whole thing, Gill?" she said.

Taylor hoped that she could talk him out of this. It would be better for all of them if they drove away.

"I need you to see," Gill said. Desperate and pleading.

Kacie turned to Taylor. "Get in."

Taylor slid into the backseat, the air in the car redolent with french fries.

As Kacie made her way to the driver's seat, Taylor looked over to Gill. "My tracks," Taylor said. "Tonight."

"You have my word."

Kacie's door slammed shut and they were all huddled in the tiny Toyota.

"Astound me," she said.

"You're never going to see me again," Taylor said. "After tonight. You won't be able to find me."

Kacie huffed. "For the best, I'm sure we can all agree."

Taylor pulled off his gloves and jammed them into his pockets. His fingers looked ghostly in the diffuse light. Before he could stop himself, he reached into the front and put his hand on Gill's shoulder. Gill's nervous system twisted and coiled under his dense skin.

"We got ourselves a hot mic," Gill said to Kacie, then he lifted his right knee up in front of him. "I'm wiggling my toes."

Kacie put both of her hands over her eyes as if watching a horror movie. A noise escaped from her, high-pitched and clipped, and she leaned away from him. With her eyes closed, her hands frantically pawed the door until she found the handle. It opened with a whoosh, and Kacie fell backward onto the ground. She scrambled away from the car like a crab.

Gill pushed himself out after her. Taylor leaned forward, over the front seat, but as soon as Gill took his first step, he lost contact and Gill fell heavily to the ground, too.

With both Gill and Kacie out of commission, Taylor knew he should run. A clean getaway. Instead, he got out and knelt next to Gill. As soon as Taylor put his hand on his shoulder, Gill hopped up with purpose.

"Kacie," he said, and Taylor followed him around the Toyota like a duckling. Kacie was now curled in a fetal position.

Fully upright, Gill's upper torso was like a kick drum. He leaned down and picked up Kacie like a small child. She nuzzled her face into his corded neck.

"I missed you, Gill."

"I've been here all along."

This was really bad. These two were rekindling something. They were going to kill Taylor before the night was over.

"I think I should go," Taylor said.

Without turning around Gill said, "Don't let go, you son of a bitch."

"I can't follow you around forever," Taylor said.

"I'm not asking for forever. I just want more time right now."

Taylor nodded even though neither of them were looking at him. "Sure, man. A few more minutes. Then we go to the studio."

"Let's dance," Gill said to Kacie, still cradled in his arms, and she responded with a primal cooing sound. Taylor was having heart palpitations. Everything was falling apart.

Gill returned Kacie to the ground where she swayed for a moment before regaining her balance. She seemed to have completely erased Taylor from the scene. Taylor and Gill moved in unison to the car. Gill leaned into the open driver door and snapped on the radio. For a moment, Taylor heard his own voice singing softly over a bowed bass. They really had been listening to his demo. But then Gill switched to a song Taylor remembered from his childhood. Maybe Whitney Houston?

Gill had also taken to pretending that Taylor wasn't there, and Taylor almost lost contact with him in his hurry to get back to Kacie.

She folded into him, and they began dancing like they were at prom and had never danced in their lives. Taylor stood behind Gill's broad back, suddenly embarrassed to be a witness.

He looked away just in time to see a slow-moving bee, definitely up past its bedtime, meandering through the air toward him. His muscles tensed and his throat constricted. The bee continued toward him, drunk or confused or both. Gill and Kacie swayed in front of him.

The bee dove toward Taylor, a lazy lunge, but it was enough for Taylor to let go of Gill's shoulder and jump to the side. Gill lurched forward. Kacie tried to catch him, but he tipped into her and the two of them fell to the pavement a second time. But this time, Gill's massive body was on top of her.

Taylor looked around frantically for the bee, but it had fled the scene.

"What the fuck?" Kacie yelled. Apparently now she could see Taylor.

"Sorry, there was a bee." He knew this was his chance to leave so he didn't move toward them.

She pushed Gill off of her in a massive show of strength, and Taylor was so stunned that he didn't move when she got to her feet and lunged at him. Her head connected with his shoulder and he spun sideways. Kacie regained her footing and kicked him in the knee.

Taylor dropped to the pavement, his hip making contact first. He rested his head against the ground and looked at Gill. Tears streamed down his cheeks.

"Sorry about that, man," Taylor said to him. "This night was going to end in tears no matter what we did."

Gill sucked in a wavering breath. "I don't want to live like this anymore."

"Maybe you don't have to," Kacie said, suddenly standing over Taylor. "Maybe I'll cut off his hands and take them with us." She kicked Taylor in the same shoulder she'd headbutted earlier and he rolled away from her. She kicked him again in the back. Pain blossomed in his spine.

"Stop kicking me," Taylor tried to say, but he was pretty sure it didn't come out that way. He rolled away again and this time she got him in the ribs. Something popped, and the agony was brutal. He tried to roll into a ball, but it was too painful.

Kacie was about to kick him in the head. Taylor could see her New Balance sneaker making its way to his mouth. But then suddenly, she was lifted into the air, her legs kicking beneath her like she was crowd surfing. She struggled against something Taylor couldn't see, screaming madly. Clearly flying against her will.

Then she was dropped on the hood of her car with a thud.

2

Denise ran across the parking lot to where Taylor writhed on the ground. "You're going to be okay," she said.

He looked skinnier than the last time she'd seen him. And now that he'd been beaten up by that rabid woman, it was hard to tell if he was always that pale or not. He tried to sit up, but she held him down.

"Don't move."

"Denise?"

She'd forgotten she was invisible. She returned to view and rubbed his head.

The woman was sprawled across the hood, breathing heavily, but had clearly calmed down. And the big man was blubbering away from his spot on the ground. They had to get out of there before the cops showed up. But she was pretty sure Taylor had some broken bones.

"What happened here?" Denise said.

Taylor tried to get up again. Denise held him down once more. "Just relax."

"What happened to your face?" Taylor said with difficulty.

"I'll tell you later."

The woman got off the car and moved next to the big man on the pavement.

"I think my rib is broken," Taylor gasped.

"Wouldn't surprise me," Beth said. Denise looked up to find Beth hovering above them, her sling pushed to the side and her cast covered in scuffs.

"That was glorious," Denise said as Beth landed lightly next to her.

"I'm not kidding," Taylor said. "I think my rib is broken."

Day Two

A DASTARDLY PLOT UNFOLDS

CHAPTER NINE

CONFUSING THE MESSAGE

1

Edna dreamt she'd died in the night. Or perhaps there were no dreams and the void had overwhelmed her. But either way, she awoke confused and tired. Thankfully, her fresh sheets weren't soiled.

"It's funny how you feel worse now that you know about me," the glioblastoma said from where it nestled in her brain.

She did feel worse. Much worse. So she didn't respond. It could probably hear her thoughts anyway.

"I sure can!"

The world tilted to the left as Edna got to her feet, and she tilted to the right to compensate. She gripped her dresser to steady herself as she took slow, deliberate steps toward the bathroom. She got through the door without further incident, but when she leaned over to start the water in the shower, the world teetered forward and she had to scramble backwards to remain upright. Her toothbrush and toothpaste and rubbing alcohol and face cream crashed to the floor as she reached for something to hold her up; finally clutching the sink faucet, her body still angled toward the shower. The water splashed pleasantly into the tub, totally oblivious to her struggle. The hardest lesson in life was learning that the universe was indifferent to every human clawing around on the surface of the Earth. Some of those humans made a mark and some of them didn't, but the universe didn't care either way. No one left a lasting impression in the end.

After a few moments of heavy breathing, she regained her balance enough to lurch into the shower. The hot water felt good on her back and shoulders. She felt her skin pinkening. If it were possible to miss things once you were dead, Edna would miss showers. And cherries jubilee ice cream.

She felt a bit steadier by the end of her shower, but she'd lost track of time completely. The water had been gradually getting colder, but she hadn't want to stop experiencing the sensation of each individual droplet pummeling her skin. Each one a reminder that she was still here and still alive and still able to receive sensory transmissions. It terrified her that she would lose that connection with her body. The body she'd always been in. The one that had curled into the folds and joints of Nolan. The body that had produced three children. The body that was now letting her down.

Edna was glad for the steam on the mirror so she didn't have to see herself. Without a reflection, she could be any age; at any time in her life. She could be the girl that Nolan had carried through the front door. The girl who'd tried to make the house feel like home. The girl who'd learned to cook from a stack of books her mom had bought her. The girl who struggled to be a mom. The girl who Nolan had left alone when he'd died. What was to be done with these memories? There was no way to store them. No way to take them with her.

She could not pull herself away. For the first time in nearly thirty years of teaching, Edna was running late.

Once she'd dressed for the day, she felt a bit more like herself. But she didn't want to run into Beth. Those sad, wide eyes were too much. Edna preferred Beth before Beth found out Edna was dying. There had always been anger between them. Blame for Nolan's death despite an uneasy truce. But now Beth wanted to be a caregiver. After Edna had banned any talk of her diagnosis at dinner last night, Beth had mooned over Edna like she was going to die any fucking second: refilling her glass multiple times and rinsing her plate after dinner. That was the thing with their family. Nolan still held them together with his inhuman strength, even from the grave.

And of course, Edna was her mother. Edna knew it must be hard to watch your mother in the process of dying. Watching someone else die reminded you it wouldn't be long before it was your turn. Edna hated being a reminder. She'd rather do other things with her remaining days.

So she moved quietly as she left her room, but, just like when Beth was young, Edna couldn't help but look into her room on her way downstairs. Beth's room was a surprising mess. The complete opposite of when Beth was a child. DVDs on the floor. A laptop open on a dresser. Clothes piled in the corner. But the strangest thing about the room was the addition of Denise. She and Beth had never really been close. And here they were entangled in the same small bed. Both fast asleep.

Denise looked worse than she had yesterday. Deep black under her eyes and her swollen lip visibly pulsed with her heartbeat. Beth was on her right side, her cast cradled against her chest. She winced in her sleep.

Edna wondered what had happened after Denise had left last night and Edna had gone off to bed. Both Denise and Beth were still in the clothes they'd been wearing, and neither were under the blanket. Must have been some party.

She pulled the door closed and tottered down the stairs. Ever since Beth had arrived, she hadn't been able to watch her special videos saved to her computer. The videos weren't exactly sexual for her. She didn't masturbate or touch herself in any way. But there was still something very private about it. Edna didn't want anyone else to know.

Since she was already running late and it appeared that nothing could wake her daughters, Edna decided to watch one before work.

And that's how she happened upon Taylor. Her son. The one she missed most of all. He breathed heavily on the couch across from her computer, a sheet twisted around his legs. His thin chest was wrapped in tight white gauze, and he sported some deep bruises on his shoulders and arms. He had quite the black eye as well. What had happened to her children? Her house had transformed into a convalescent home in the night.

Edna wanted to sit at the edge of the couch and cradle him in her arms. She wanted to make his pain go away. Not just the visible stuff. But all the pain swimming inside him. If only she could leave this life knowing that Taylor was sorted out. That he'd forgiven himself for what had happened with that girl all those years ago. That he'd allow himself to be happy again. To know that he deserved it. Edna wanted happiness for all of her children. You get such little access to true happiness in this life. Why did they all spend so much time avoiding it?

"Your children are going to take over your house when you're gone and they are going to fuck it up royally," the tumor said.

"Probably," Edna said. "But I'll be dead. I'll have no idea."

It had been over a year since she'd seen Taylor, and Edna hoped he'd still be at the house when she returned from school later. It would be nice to talk to him.

She didn't watch any videos.

Edna arrived at the school without much memory of the drive. She didn't remember grabbing the Sherlock Holmes book for Phillip either, but there it was on the passenger seat. She reclined her seat, cracked the window and stared out the windshield at a thin cloud hovering above the school. Her eyes suddenly felt loose in their sockets. Her jaw ached.

Then a ripple. Like time had folded in on itself, and then there was Hank at the window staring down at her. Her hands were clenched into fists.

"I think you had a seizure, Edna," Hank said, as if he'd seen it happen a million times.

"I don't think so."

"Either way, you might want to see a doctor."

Edna rubbed her wrists and knuckles while trying to focus on Hank's overly concerned face. "I'm fine. What are you doing here anyway?"

"I was running late, and I saw you sitting in your car. That was something I'd never seen before. You're usually the first one here."

Edna leaned forward and rolled the window the rest of the way down. A breeze pushed past Hank and danced across her cheeks and through her hair. She tried not to look directly into his eyes.

"I'm sorry about yesterday," she said. "That was unforgivable. I feel like a creep."

His face colored along the cheekbones. "Well. It's only unforgivable if I didn't like it."

"It's not right to grab someone the way I grabbed you."

"Let's agree to disagree on that and move on," Hank said. "Because it was wonderful. I want to do it again. I want to do more. We don't have time for decorum." He inhaled deeply, filling his chest with something that might resemble passion. Edna hadn't seen that in a long, long time. "I want you in my life," he said. "Not just at school or a quick chat in the parking lot. We could be there for each other. We could intertwine our lives."

"I'm dying, Hank."

Hank nearly crumpled. "You don't have to say that, Edna. I understand if you don't want to take this any further."

"I have a brain tumor. I just found out. I'll be dead by the end of the year."

Hank leaned against her car, his midsection filling the entire window. "You're serious."

"I wish I wasn't. I'm starting to feel ill-prepared for it."

Hank snorted. Not quite a laugh, more of an understanding. He rested his elbows on the car door and met her gaze.

Edna looked away again. It was too much. This little nugget of proffered happiness in her final days. "Trust me, Hank. I'd like to fuck you. I've been watching quite a lot of pornography."

He inhaled forcefully and she heard the spit gather in his throat. "I do too, Edna. I've never told anyone."

"But we can't do this. I don't want you feeling we're at the start of something special, and then I leave you. Just like Monica."

Hank swallowed loudly and rocked on his feet. "All morning I was thinking about what Monica would say about us getting together."

"What did you decide?"

"I think she would approve. But I only determined that this very moment."

"You miss her."

"So much, Edna. I miss her more every day."

"I miss Nolan. Of course, I do. But I'm finally not angry at him anymore. That's the important thing I learned. If you're doing life correctly, someone will be pissed off when you die. I was that person for Nolan. And I appreciate my role now. It's important."

Hank nodded. "I will be pissed when you die. That we waited this long and now we can't do anything about it."

"That's the spirit, Hank."

"I mean it, Edna."

"I know you do." She reached over to the passenger seat and grabbed the Sherlock Holmes book. "Will you give this to Phillip for me?"

"Sure. But aren't you coming in?"

"I don't think so." She looked up again at the thin cloud above the school. "I don't think I'll be going in there ever again."

2

Crunching. Incessant crunching. Like a three-part harmony. Four different boxes of cereal on the table. Beth remembered she still had a few leftover Pop Tarts in her room, but the mere thought of them caused a chain reaction of memory that started at the grocery store and ended with her at the bottom of the stairs. In response, Beth's left arm spasmed with pain. She dropped her spoon and clutched the cast.

Taylor slurped his milk loudly and winced as he leaned back in his chair. He adjusted the body wrap that he'd acquired in the emergency room. "Your face is making my face hurt," he said to Denise.

"Now you know how I feel. Your face has always bothered me." Denise took a dainty bite of cereal, careful not to open her mouth too wide.

Beth figured she better jump in. "I can't believe that lady broke your rib, Taylor."

Taylor shifted again, but still couldn't seem to get comfortable. "She was probably mad I'd only recorded five songs. She was desperate for more."

Another chasm revealed. Beth had never heard a song Taylor had recorded. Like ever.

"Can I hear them too?" Beth said.

"I wish. You two swooped in last night and dragged me away from the only people who can give me my final masters."

"I actually think we saved your life," Denise said. "That lady was going to kill you if Beth didn't pull her off of you."

"I was handling it."

"I think she was handling you." As hard as she tried, Denise couldn't help laughing at her own joke. She reflexively reached for her bruised cheeks and lip.

"We're a sorry group," Beth said. "You'd think we were the ones dying."

That brought the rising tension down as each of them thought about Mom in their own way. Or so Beth presumed.

Denise picked up a box of cereal and then thought better of it and put it down. "It's weird you can't heal yourself," she said to Taylor. "I never thought about it until now."

Taylor shrugged. "I'm always in contact with me. Even if sometimes I'd like a break. But yeah. I can't do anything about this broken rib or food poisoning or a paper cut. Just gotta ride it out like every other sucker."

Then the doorbell rang. And Beth knew exactly who it was. She felt the hesitancy in the actual sound of the bell ringing. She could picture Renata shrinking away from the door. Maybe wishing she'd talked herself out of this.

"I need you to heal me," Beth said. "Right now."

"I'm busy," Taylor said and shifted in his chair.

"This is serious. I can't have a broken arm right now."

"Well, I can't have a broken rib right now."

"Wait," Denise said. "Is that her?"

"She can't know I broke my arm." Beth gave Taylor her most pleading look. He looked exhausted. Washed out. Diminished. Maybe they had ruined his chance at finishing his EP.

"You help me with this," Beth said. "And Denise and I will help you get your recording masters."

"Wait. What? How?" Denise said.

The doorbell rang again. Beth could feel the confidence returning. Renata was ready to talk now.

"Deal." Taylor grunted loudly as he got to his feet. He pulled off his glove and pressed his palm onto Beth's back. He'd only ever healed her once before, when they were both still young. It had surprised her then and it surprised her again now. It wasn't only that her arm was healed. It was everything about her. All the pieces snapped back into place. Her confidence. Her well-being. Her happiness. She was the best person she would ever be. And the comedown would be hard when she realized she couldn't be this person without assistance. That the best form of herself was unattainable.

"Wipe the smile off your face and let's go answer that door," Taylor said. But he grinned a little. Or winced. It was hard to tell.

Beth quickly pulled off the sling, her arm moving better than she ever thought possible. Like she could be an Olympic swimmer. Or a baseball pitcher. Or someone who lifted their arm up and down a lot. She ripped into the cast and began pulling it apart. It took all three of them cursing and swearing to remove the cast from her arm. Then she and Taylor maneuvered to the door like they were in a potato sack race, making sure they never lost contact with each other.

Taylor yanked open the door just as Renata got to the end of the walkway. She looked slight but brimming with power. It was hard for Beth not to be in love with her.

"I'm here," Beth said out of breath, but buoyant. Elated.

"You need to settle down a little," Taylor whispered.

Renata turned toward them. "I thought you were maybe ignoring me. I'm really sorry about yesterday."

She peered at Beth intently. Taking her in. Looking for a crack.

"I'm not mad," Beth said.

Renata peered at her. "Are you okay? All night I kept thinking you were hurt. It was eating me up inside. I should have stayed at the hospital with you."

Beth opened her arms wide. "Perfect working order."

Taylor laughed, and Renata finally nodded to him. "Who's this?"

"Oh sorry. This is my brother. My sister and I went to pick him up last night because my mom is dying."

Taylor nudged her with his other arm, but Beth knew she couldn't say one wrong thing. She was at the top of her game.

"Oh, Beth, I'm sorry to hear that."

"We're still in shock."

Renata shook her head sadly. "I bet."

"I recognize you," Taylor said. "Didn't you do all the school plays? Everyone thought you were weird."

"Not everyone," Beth said.

"I thought you were hot," Taylor said.

"Oh," Renata said.

"I think you're hot too," Beth said.

"Oh," Renata said again and pivoted away from them, her arms swinging awkwardly. "You both are good-looking as well."

Another wave of well-being suffused Beth. "I got nervous when you reached out to touch me. I'm going through a break-up. I'm scared of feelings."

"Feelings?" Renata said. "I think maybe…" She looked at Taylor. "It's nice to meet you, Taylor, but can we talk privately, Beth?"

Beth wanted nothing more than to talk privately with Renata. But… "My brother and I are really close," Beth said.

"Very close," Taylor said.

"I see that," Renata said. "Like literally close. You're almost standing in the same spot."

Something slithered into Beth's euphoric brain. Doubt.

"We just found out about our mom last night," Beth said. Was there any way to explain their strange behavior?

"I understand," Renata said. "I just thought we might want to talk for a minute. Just the two of us."

"Yes. We can do that. But can it be later? Another time? Please tell me this won't be the last time I see you."

"It won't," Renata said.

"Sounds like we cleared this up then," Taylor said and bestowed them both with his broadest smile. "All a big misunderstanding."

"Yeah," Beth said.

"Yeah," Renata said.

Then Taylor pulled Beth inside.

3

Of course, the only option was to pretend like he still had a job, or else Phillip would finally discover John's propensity for failing. He put on his work clothes and drove Phillip to school. He was still raw about Phillip running off last night. John knew it was silly, especially considering that Phillip didn't know about anything that happened, but that didn't stop John from driving in total silence. He'd even driven away before making sure Phillip had gotten through the front of the school, which he'd never done before. But guilt had pushed him to drive around the circle one more time to double check, confident that his point had been made. Though he wondered if Phillip noticed the little things that John did.

When he got home, he sat in the driveway and considered his dilapidated house. He should use the time off to mow the lawn, plant some bushes under the front windows, pressure-wash the windows. He imagined what it must have looked like to Denise. How disappointed she must have been in the whole experience. He pulled her number out of his wallet and realized that it was surely fake. He'd only know if he called, but he didn't want to know yet. John wasn't sure if he'd ever want to know.

But now he was also faced with the realization that he didn't know what to do with himself at all. He didn't like this feeling of listlessness. Maybe with his day free he could try out some old hobbies. Like video games. Or Pokémon cards. Or masturbation.

He could dig out his collection of Maxim magazines and a few old Linda Fiorentino movies from the back of his closet. And a Playboy he'd stolen from his dad in the 90s. Not a stunning "porn" collection, but they could do the trick.

John hardly masturbated because he was convinced he'd be caught every time. By Phillip or one of the neighbors or a Jehovah's Witness or a low flying satellite or worst of all, the ghost of his dead mother or father. Not just during the act, but also after. As if some indication of what he'd done lingered on him for hours afterward.

But the neighborhood seemed eerily quiet today. As if everyone was waiting to see what he was going to do. Of course, he should be applying for jobs. John knew that. He got out of the car and walked up to the porch.

Then he stopped. Some animal sixth sense buried in his DNA told him something wasn't right. There was a presence that hadn't been there when he'd left. He shuddered.

He could turn and leave. Let the presence take over his home. He and Phillip could move away. Live in hotels. In the back of the car. Or John could finally stand up to something. He could fight for the life he wanted.

The front door was unlocked even though John knew he'd locked it on the way out. He straightened his back. Clenched his fists. Buried his fear.

Entered his house.

Molly sat on the couch, scrolling through her phone as if she'd never left.

"Smells like cabbage in here," she said as if John constantly returned home to find her sitting there. "Did you cook cabbage?"

He opened his mouth, but no words came out.

"I couldn't believe my key still worked," she said and put her phone in her pocket. "I hope you don't mind I let myself in. I didn't feel like sitting outside."

She somehow looked more beautiful than John remembered. Age had changed her in lovely ways; her hips slightly broader, her face rounder. But she had the same high cheekbones and prominent collarbone. She wore a simple flowered dress that revealed her tan legs from the knees down. Her manicured toenails poked from her sandals.

"You look great," Molly said, plucking the words he'd planned to say to her.

John took a step forward and she got up from the couch, her hair resting on her shoulders. He'd never seen her hair that long, and he desperately wanted to grab two handfuls of it.

"Is that really you?" John said. He didn't care how stupid it sounded. He needed to know.

She ducked her head and shimmied toward him. "Yes, it's me."

And then their lips rammed together as if they were magnetized. Her pointed tongue found his as he struggled to take air in through his nose. They grappled each other like old enemies. Like a much-hyped rematch. They pushed at each other's face and arms and hips, trying to see who would bruise first.

John wanted to crush her and chew her and spit her out. He wanted to dismember her and force her into the garbage disposal. He wanted her to feel the pain he'd kept hidden.

She threw him onto the couch, her hands undoing his belt and forcing his pants down to his ankles. John hiked up her dress and ripped her underwear from her thighs, the right strap snapping with the force. He let go and they slid gracefully down her left leg as heat poured from between her legs. He pressed his face against the dark brittle hair and inhaled deeply. It was like returning to the earth, like being buried.

Molly pushed his face away, and he banged the back of his head against the couch. She dug her nails into his chest and straddled him. Sweat glistened on her arms. She bucked her hips and knocked all of the wind from his lungs.

John fought back. He slapped both of her arms away and pulled her dress down. Her nipples were so hard they felt as though they'd break his teeth. But that didn't stop him from biting on the left one until she yelped with pain. She reached around behind her and smacked his balls. Tears sprung to John's eyes, and he coughed loudly. She leaned backward, her body so hot that he thought she would burn him.

"You're not even hard," she whispered.

"What?" But she was right. He focused on his cock, and he found it curled into his abdomen as if he'd been swimming in an ice-cold pool.

She slumped off of him, rolling onto her back and reclining next to him on the couch; their shoulders touching. She gently pulled up her dress.

"That's never happened before," John said.

"Your body knows more than you do. This is a bad idea. It's not like we're going to get back together. Raise our son together. Forget the last ten years ever happened."

"I know."

She breathed heavily.

"I really wanted to fuck you," he said.

"Me, too."

"Well, technically, you already fucked me. When you ran off."

Molly sighed. "Technically, I fucked myself then too."

Their chests heaved in unison. The closeness of Molly was so strange, so alien, that John laughed to assign it some meaning.

Molly laughed too.

"Why?" John said. A massive, all-encompassing, all-caps WHY that covered their courtship and marriage and unplanned parenthood and the abrupt dissolution of the pact they'd made.

"After Phillip was born, I found myself with a child, sure, but no C-section scar. No stretch marks. After a few months, you couldn't tell I'd ever carried another human being to term. It was like it never happened, which, if I'm honest, is what I kind of wanted. My options were to stay here with you and keep popping out babies or use this second chance I was given."

"Second chance?" John said.

"To make it." Molly shifted away from him. "I'd spent nine months knowing, just knowing, that this baby was going to ruin my chances at an acting career."

Hearing it laid out so bluntly, in a way that John had always pushed back against, hurt him incredibly. Molly had missed the point of everything. That building a life wasn't about succeeding on your own.

"It didn't work out, as you probably know," Molly said. "And it probably gives you great joy knowing I failed."

John shook his head. "It doesn't."

"Now I'm even thinking of trying to marry a rich guy. Basically, I hate myself. As you can imagine." She looked at him. "Are you crying?"

"I don't like this story," John said.

"Think how I feel." Molly laughed again, but it rang hollowly in the room.

"Why didn't you talk to me?" John said.

"We were past that point in our relationship. There was no going back. But I saw how happy you were. How much you loved Phillip. I was an unneeded appendage."

"You're needed."

Molly sat up. "That's what I was hoping. That's why I'm here. Stop crying."

"I've been holding it in," John said. "I'm just going to let it play out." He let a couple of sobs that felt good all over. Molly rubbed his back and he felt himself getting hard. He wasn't going back down that path.

"I'm here because he called me," she said. "I'm here because I think we both want to be in each other's lives."

"Why don't you come out to dinner with us," John said. "He loves going to that steak place with the soft serve machine."

"You mean the place where you asked me to marry you?"

"Yeah. But we never sit at that table."

Molly stopped rubbing his back and stood up. She picked up the remnants of her underwear and adjusted her dress. "This place is kind of depressing," she said. "Nothing has changed."

"Phillip has changed considerably," John said with a small amount of venom. He still wanted to hurt her.

"Let's do dinner," she said. "But can I pick him up from school? I'd love to have some time just the two of us. We'll meet you there."

That feeling came back. The one John had felt at the door. Like he knew something was wrong. "I don't even think the school will let you."

Molly frowned at him. "You could call though, right? Tell them his mom is going to pick him up." She looked away from him, blocking her face. "I've never called myself that before. Mom."

John wanted to say she didn't deserve to be called a mom. She hadn't earned it yet. Not until she'd sat up with Phillip when he had a fever. Cut gum out of his hair. Tied his shoes in the middle of a soccer game. She wasn't a mom.

"I'll give the school a call," John said. "See what I can do."

CHAPTER TEN

MUDDLING THE PROGRESS

1

Denise felt adrift. She couldn't go back to her apartment, because she hadn't paid rent in two months. Plus, the last two nights she hadn't even slept in her own bed. She'd stayed a pleasant night with John and then the worst sleep of her life with Beth, and by now, her roommate probably thought she'd bailed completely. Which might be for the best. Everyone else seemed to be moving in with Mom, maybe it was Denise's turn too.

But she couldn't take any more Taylor and Beth today. She'd left them to continue bickering about inconsequential stuff instead of talking about their mom. She'd gotten up and walked out the door without a word to either of them. Possible they hadn't even noticed. After the initial warmth she'd felt when she'd seen them all assembled at the table that morning, Denise just wanted to be alone. Plus, her face hurt so badly it seemed like her skull was losing its shape and folding in on itself.

So she went out on patrol for the first time in years.

Patrol was a way for Denise to atone. An opportunity to use her power for good. She couldn't remember the last time she'd done it. There was just the fog of past patrols, all of them a bust, blending into each other and leaving no distinguishable mark. Nothing ever happened. Not once. It wasn't like in the movies when Batman drove into Gotham and then boom, there was a bank robbery, or a mugging, or some super villain rising to power for him to thwart. There were people milling around and going into strip malls and eating fast food and filling up their gas tanks.

Today was different though. She didn't want to make up for all the times she'd stolen wallets or clothes or food. Denise was chasing the thrill she'd experienced last night during Taylor's rescue. That pure smack of adrenaline. When she'd awoken this morning, she expected all three of them to be buzzing from it. Instead, she'd found the same surly Beth and whatever this defeated version of Taylor was. Didn't they realize what they'd accomplished? What they could still do? This was how they could send Mom off without regrets. Their mom could finally see them embracing who they really were. The powers that each of them had gotten from their dad, no longer a liability, but something to be cherished and nurtured.

Also, Denise kind of wanted to beat people up. As long as they were the bad guys.

So, patrol wasn't about balancing the scales anymore. It was about righting the wrongs of the world and giving herself over to a higher cause. Her power was meant to help people.

Two hours later, it was also boring as fuck.

It was exactly as she remembered. Even that leftover drip of adrenaline couldn't push Denise through hours of watching people go about their day. Life was so tedious. People drove their cars and parked their cars and walked into buildings and walked out of buildings. They carried bags. Some of them tucked in their shirts. Some of them didn't. Hardly anyone spoke to each other. If there were interactions, pleasantries were usually involved. Or someone was allowing another person to walk ahead of them or holding a door or lifting a heavy item for an elderly person or returning their shopping carts to the cart corrals or paying someone a compliment. Meanwhile, Denise was right there. She could turn invisible, and nobody, nobody, nobody needed her to do it.

She craved the elation she'd experience if she invisibly clotheslined a purse snatcher or tied a bank robber's shoelaces together or infiltrated the mob. But did people still snatch purses? When had she ever heard of a bank robbery in her town? And who was she kidding, the only mob around was the local school board. Denise would settle for solving a parking spot dispute or returning a cell phone someone left on the table in a restaurant. But she couldn't manifest anything.

And there in her car after hours of patrolling, she felt it again. Failure. So much failure.

You know what was easier than looking for crime? Being the criminal. That was always the truth. It was still the truth. Denise wanted to use her power, but she only knew how to steal and get herself out of the dubious situations in which she landed herself.

That's why she couldn't make a connection with someone like John. One-night stand? All the way. Maybe even a two-night stand. But anything more required revelations.

Denise got out of her car and turned invisible. She purposefully brushed past a few people on her way down the sidewalk. Just like when she was visible. A mild annoyance to all those around her.

She went into the grocery store and grabbed a cart, startling an old couple. Denise reappeared for a moment and smiled at them. She gripped the cart and disappeared again, this time taking the cart with her. The old man clutched the old woman and Denise knew her good deed for the day was getting their heart rates up.

Denise set off into the aisles, mining the exhilarating drops of last night. God it was incredible. The way she and Beth had turned from Taylor's apartment and somehow saw Taylor there, following that couple around. Then the shocking moment when the woman had turned and attacked him. The way Denise and Beth launched into action as if they had done it a million times. Denise jumping onto Beth's back and turning them both invisible, and then that sickening but incredible lurch into the air as Beth propelled them toward the parking lot. Beth diving towards the woman and Denise jumping down gracefully and shoving her off of Taylor. Without missing a beat, Beth grabbing her by the shoulders and flying backwards to the car to drop her heavily on the hood.

Electricity buzzed through Denise as she pushed the cart up and down the aisles. How could she do that again? She needed to do that again. Getting the tracks for Taylor's EP was child's play. Denise wanted to get physical.

She let go of the cart near the deli meats and it reappeared before crashing into a display of cheeses. A few people looked up. Nobody cared.

Denise moved next to a woman and knocked a loaf of bread from the shelf. The woman picked it up. What would it feel like to go to John's house tonight and show him what she could do?

Denise reappeared to the world in the cereal aisle and not a single person noticed. She left without stealing anything. It was time to head back to the house.

She was sure there was a crime happening somewhere in their town, but patrol was officially over. Denise started her car and for the first time wondered what it might be like to date a police officer or a detective. If she got the inside scoop, she might be able to really help. Just the idea sparked a little of that exhilaration she'd felt earlier.

Then she pulled out into the street and found herself behind her mom's car. Shouldn't she still be at school? Why was she here across town?

Denise tried to maneuver to get next to her, but the car in the next lane wouldn't let her in. The light up ahead turned green and suddenly her mom's car jumped forward and rammed the car in front of her. But even though her mom's car had stopped, the motor continued to rev loudly as if it was going to suddenly drive over the other car.

Something had happened to her mom.

Denise jumped out of her car and never once thought to turn invisible.

2

Phillip watched the substitute teacher. A short man with long hair and glasses. He walked flat-footed like a hobbit. He wrote on the board while standing on tiptoes. He had no interest in learning anyone's name. He just kept pointing and saying things like "second row, third seat" as if the students' placement in the room defined them.

What Phillip was trying to discover was if the substitute teacher knew anything. If there was anything to give away, Phillip was going to catch it. A hint of sadness in the way he sat in Mrs. Clark's chair. A forlorn glance at the students. A hesitancy in his movements.

Basically, Phillip needed to detect if Mrs. Clark had died in the night. And if this strange man in their classroom wouldn't tell them with his body language, Phillip planned to ask him bluntly before the end of the day.

Phillip's chest ached from the cigarettes he'd had with Suz last night, but he knew it was more than that. It was knowing that Mrs. Clark was going to die. That his dad was lonelier and sadder than he'd ever expected. That he'd seen Mrs. Clark's daughter disappear. But the more events that accumulated between that moment and the present, the less he trusted his memory. Phillip wanted magic in the world, but he also wanted it to make sense. Maybe part of growing up was realizing that his dad was just a messed-up guy and sometimes you have to look the other way when something truly extraordinary happened.

The door to the room whooshed open, and Phillip looked up with more hope than he expected. The ache in his chest wanted to see Mrs. Clark there, back from whatever had kept her away that morning. But Mr. Scully was there, with that same sad face he always wore. There was no way to tell if he knew anything.

"Sorry to interrupt," Mr. Scully said. "I need to pull Phillip for a moment."

Phillip jumped up, his heart sending blood to his head so quickly that he almost fell over.

Mr. Scully looked at him strangely for a moment, his bulky eyebrows lowering. Then he waved a hand, and Phillip followed him into the hallway.

Phillip was nervous now, and his kneecaps jiggled. Now that the truth might be presenting itself, he wasn't sure he wanted to hear it.

"You know, don't you?" Mr. Scully said.

"Know what, Mr. Scully?" Phillip managed to say with no saliva in his mouth.

Mr. Scully tapped something in his hands, and it was the first time Phillip noticed he was holding a book. The exact book that Mrs. Clark tried to give him last night. The one with the detective.

"Did she...?" Phillip trailed off because he couldn't bring himself to say any words that might bring about an answer.

Mr. Scully's face softened. "No, Phillip. I saw her this morning. She wanted me to give you this book."

Phillip nodded, but he hadn't taken the book yet.

"Will it be soon?" Phillip said.

"I'm afraid it might be."

"That's what I thought."

"She wants you to have this."

Phillip nodded again.

"Have you read any of these stories before?" Mr. Scully asked.

"No."

"Want to know a secret?"

"Yes."

Mr. Scully smiled. "Neither have I."

Phillip now took the book. He imagined he could feel some part of Mrs. Clark on the cover. That they were somehow connected.

"Will she be coming back to school?" Phillip said.

"I don't think so."

"So, I'll never see her again?"

Mr. Scully knelt in front of him. "Perhaps not. But she's there in that book. When you read it, it'll be like she's reading it to you."

"Will you tell her something for me?"

"Of course."

"Tell her I saw her daughter. I know what her talent is."

Mr. Scully tilted his head. "That's kind of a strange message."

"Maybe," Phillip said. He wasn't exactly sure why he'd said it, but it seemed very much like if he wanted any chance of talking to her again, that might be the only way. "But will you tell her?"

Mr. Scully got to his feet. "Of course. I'll make sure to tell her."

A door opened down the hall, and Ms. Noon began walking towards them, forcefully, like she always did, as if she'd plow over any kid who got in her way. She stopped next to Mr. Scully and pursed her lips in her version of a smile.

"Sorry to interrupt, Mr. Scully," she said, but didn't look all that sorry. "I have a message for you, Phillip. Your dad called."

His knees suddenly felt weak again. "Is he okay?"

"Yes. He wanted me to pass along a message. Your mom is going to pick you up today."

Phillip's heart stopped, all of his blood standing still in his veins. He felt completely removed from the hallway and the school and the whole town. Like he was suddenly an inert satellite orbiting his own life.

"You okay?" Mr. Scully said as he picked up the book that Phillip had apparently dropped.

"Who's picking me up?" Phillip asked.

Ms. Noon turned toward her office door and began her aggressive walk. "Your mom, Phillip. Your mom is going to pick you up. Isn't that nice?"

3

Beth's arm hurt like a bitch. She had put it back in the sling, but she understood now why doctors put casts on broken parts. Every slight move sent new spasms of pain.

"One more hit?" Beth said to Taylor who was now reclining on the couch.

"You have to come to me."

"But it hurts when I move."

"It hurts when I move too," Taylor said. "Seems like you have a tough decision to make."

It had been so long since she'd been in the same room with Taylor that she was having a hard time connecting with him. They seemed comfortable poking fun at each other, or Denise, but the years apart had loosened any closeness they used to have.

"What do you think she meant?" Beth said.

"Oh man. I knew you were going to obsess over that," Taylor said.

"I think maybe…" Beth said, repeating the three undecipherable words that Renata had uttered in response to the transference of feelings.

Taylor grunted. "Conjecture never helps."

"I'll never rest until I know what she meant."

"You could ask her."

"Then she'll know how much I care."

"You could get a lobotomy."

"Absolutely. Perfect plan."

Beth got up from the chair, wincing the whole time, and sat down on the floor next to the couch. Taylor leaned over and placed his hand on her shoulder. The relief was immediate. Her brain pushed the pain out as if her arm had never been broken. The self-doubt dissipated and she could ponder without hating herself.

"I think maybe… I gave you the wrong impression," Beth said.

"Perfectly plausible. Or… I think maybe we're moving too fast."

"Oooh," Beth said. "I like that one."

Taylor shifted with a groan. "I think maybe I'm not gay."

Beth laughed. "No. More likely I think maybe I am gay."

"So you say to her that you think she's hot. That there's feelings. And maybe that turns her gay?"

"Yes, it's that easy," Beth said with another laugh. "We should probably stop because I feel too good considering everything that is going on."

Beth steadied her arm as Taylor took his palm from her shoulder and the pain and uncertainty cascaded over her.

"Tell me about your music," Beth said.

"No," Taylor said.

"I didn't know you were still trying."

"Trying? It's the only thing I have."

"What do you do when it doesn't work out?"

"Not an option."

"But aren't you too old now? Hasn't the moment passed?"

"Just because you don't have dreams doesn't mean other people don't as well, Beth."

That one cut all the way through. She was severed in half. Beth immediately thought of Fran and how much the promotion to Director of their department meant to her. She'd been passed over twice before. "Once because I'm a woman. Once because I'm Black. I'm afraid that I will be passed over a third time because I'm gay." Sitting here with Taylor with a broken arm and broken thoughts, Beth finally understood Fran's motivations and her desires. In her career, long before Beth came along, she had goals and setbacks and near misses, but she still dreamed. Fran wanted more for herself, and she got it. She'd pursued Beth too. Brought her into her dream orbit. And all Beth wanted was to do as little work as possible, watch a bunch of movies, and bemoan the fact that someone hadn't given her a film career even though she'd never done anything to deserve it. Then, in a final selfish act, when Fran had gone out with the head of the department to celebrate the promotion and hadn't invited Beth, she'd grabbed her stuff and left.

"You're a dick," Beth said.

"It's very true."

"I'm not only upset at myself," Beth said. "I'm sad about Mom too."

"I feel depleted thinking about all the years we kept to ourselves," Taylor said. "We can't get any of the time back and it's not like any of us grew or became better people on our own."

"I know I didn't." Fran hadn't called in a day now. There was probably no way to smooth that over. And here she was obsessing over someone who was apparently super straight and just admitting that caused Beth to blush in embarrassment right there next to Taylor.

"Thanks for rescuing me," Taylor said.

"I wish I could heal you. Take your pain away too."

Taylor sighed. "When I was lying there and that woman was kicking me over and over, there was a part of me that felt satisfied. Like I'd been waiting my whole life for that moment. Like I deserved it. Also, it was the exact tempo of my favorite Radiohead song."

What if Beth had stuck around? What if instead of fleeing familial responsibility she'd stepped up and stayed strong for Taylor? Would he be sitting on the couch behind her saying that he'd been waiting for an insane woman to break his rib? Or possibly worse?

"I've made mistakes," Taylor said. "A lot of them. But I was doing something important with that guy. I felt like an artist for the first time. Then the universe was telling me that I didn't deserve it in the form of multiple kicks to the ribs."

"What if she'd killed you?"

"That was a possible next phase for sure. But I don't think so."

"So you were looking for enlightenment from an ass beating?"

Taylor actually smiled. "It sounds stupid when you say it like that. But yeah."

"We have to get your tracks."

Taylor put his feet up and lay back on the couch. "You know, Renata can be your friend. She doesn't have to be a girlfriend. You don't need to destroy every relationship that you forge."

"Like I said. Total dick," Beth said, not because he was wrong but because it was so perceptive that it was the only appropriate response.

"Don't worry. I know."

Beth wanted to give him a hard time for using the word forge like he lived in Middle Earth or something. She wanted to tell him that he didn't know anything about her life or her friends. But it would sound false coming out of her mouth. So for once, she kept it closed.

Taylor squeezed her shoulder and she leaned her head onto the couch. She flexed the fingers on her broken arm. She thought of Renata coming back to the house to check on her. Taylor was right about that too. She would be her friend.

The front door opened.

"Beth!" Denise called.

"We're in here."

Denise entered the front room, her bruised face covered in a sheen of sweat. "Mom's in the hospital."

How could it be happening already? Beth hadn't made anything right yet. Not a single thing.

CHAPTER ELEVEN

DITCHING THE PRECONCEIVED NOTIONS

1

John thought of how many cups of coffee he would have gotten for Brad Green by now. How many copies of legal documents he would have made. How many sly insinuations that John had a small dick. How many overt accusations that John had a small dick. How many times he'd be referred to as Small Dick. John wasn't happy to be jobless, but he could at least appreciate he'd never have to work that particular job again.

He had managed to masturbate after Molly left, but it wasn't a joyful experience. He tried to think of Denise, but he kept recalling her new bruised and painful-looking incarnation. Then Molly would appear and he'd have to stop because he couldn't give her the satisfaction of finishing when she was in frame, even if she couldn't possibly know about it in real life. In the end, he managed to fixate on a woman eating a large spoonful of yogurt in an ad on the back of a coupon book he'd gotten in the mail.

When he was done, he wished he hadn't bothered.

He took a hot shower and then stared at the maw of the afternoon ahead of him. But the more he stared, the more it transformed into something bigger than just the maw of the day. It was the maw of his life. It was here to swallow him. It was here to tell him that he meant nothing. And if John wasn't careful, it was going to swallow Phillip too. There was something comforting about knowing where his own life was heading. The inevitability of failure. But he couldn't allow Phillip to have the same fate. So he had to fail a little less. John wanted to believe he could accomplish that, but he wasn't totally sure.

First, he had to get through this dinner tonight. He had to make it clear to Molly that it was not okay that she'd abandoned them. Sure, Phillip was curious about her, had even memorized her phone number and called her when he'd needed help, but he and Phillip were a team. They had an unbreakable bond. Molly wasn't going to be moving back in or trying to take Phillip away.

Once that was settled, he had to tell Phillip what was going on. Phillip needed to know that John had no job. That tough times were coming. More cereal dinners. Fewer evenings out. Maybe some days without cable or power.

They'd been lucky, if you could call it luck, that when John's parents had died, they'd gotten the house they lived in and some money. But John never made enough to stop dipping into that inheritance, and now, when they really needed a little something in the bank, they had nothing. It would probably take a while to lose the house, but it wouldn't take long to lose his dignity. There had to be some other menial job out there that he was moderately qualified for. He would find it and he would take it and he would work there for years even if they spent every day demoralizing him. He would refill their coffers with extra money. Anything he could put aside. And it was imperative that he accomplished this without Phillip being embarrassed of him. There was a possible future out there where everything wasn't complete shit. But he couldn't imagine a way forward with someone like Denise. There wasn't a plan that included her. Why would anyone board the Titanic after it had already struck the iceberg?

John's first decision as a maw avoider wasn't to begin searching for jobs or looking around the house for things he could sell or even trying to tidy the place up. He went out to his car, which was dangerously low on gas, and he drove out of his neighborhood and across town to sit with the only person who had ever understood him.

His parents' gravesite was small. Two plaques embedded in perfectly green grass surrounded by hundreds of similar looking plots. John had his problems with his dad, but his mom was a true genius. She would be the first person to declare that she knew everything, but everyone who knew her claimed the same thing, so it was kind of endearing to hear her go on and on about her amazing powers of deduction.

John lay on the ground between them, his back to his father, and watched an ant crawl to the tip of a blade of grass. It perched there, its antenna curling in front of it, a lone scout searching for a better life.

"You done fucked up," his mom said. Direct and to the point as always.

"It does appear that way," John said.

"No sense trying to fix the broken lines that led you here. Look ahead. See where you want to get from here and what you have to do to get there."

"Look ahead?"

The ant looked at John as if to say, "You talking to me?"

"Ahead," his mom said. "Back is where you fucked up. Ahead is where you fix it."

The ant walked down the blade of grass and disappeared.

"What?" John said to it. "You don't think I'll fix it?"

John rolled down his windows and turned off the engine. Across the street, the school looked like a prison. Tiny windows. Cement facade. Only the one door in the front, that in recent years remained locked during the day.

A line of cars formed in the circle drive, parents waiting to pick up the children who didn't ride in the idling buses in the adjacent parking lot. He wished he'd known what kind of car Molly was driving so he could figure out if she was there, waiting anxiously for her reunion with the son she didn't even know. Would she recognize him when he walked out? It seemed unlikely.

John felt antsy in the car, his legs aching with a desire to get to Phillip before Molly did. He got out as the bell rang and jogged across the street. He reached the grass as the doors flung open and the first paroled students ran eagerly into the daylight. Within moments, it was a swarm.

He walked past the line of cars, looking into the windows, hoping to make eye contact with Molly. Wanting her to know that he was going to get to Phillip before she did.

But then there she was, standing between two buses. Gliding past the on-rushing children like she was walking through a waterfall. Before John had even hit the sidewalk leading to the front door, she staggered. The children parted around her and now Phillip was standing before her. His shoulders shook. He took a step forward, then a step back. Molly got back to her feet and reached out her hand.

Phillip took it.

Then the mass of children surrounded them again. John was running now. Trying to catch them. He caught sight of them as they passed to the other side of the buses. To a small Nissan parked in the teacher's lot. Of course, Molly parked in the teacher's lot.

They were in the car. They were driving away. Entropy increased the further he got from his car. Random images assaulted him. He needed to stop moving. So he did. He took three lungfuls of air and then he was running again. Back to his car, as Molly and Phillip drove out of the parking lot. Turning onto the street.

Driving away from him. Driving into the unblemished future.

2

Everybody in his family was totally fucked up. And not in a fun way. Taylor couldn't watch them hook up his mom to all those wires and hoses and cords, so he'd gone outside, away from the main doors, to where the faded benches were smeared with tar. The smell of recent cigarettes hovered around him like a bubble. The place where his kind of people hung out when they came to the hospital. Like, I know someone in my family is dying, but I need a fucking cigarette. Right now.

Unfortunately, Taylor didn't have any cigarettes. Not that breathing was currently his favorite activity. Even though the doctor had bound his entire chest, anything but a shallow breath made Taylor feel as if he was snapping his ribs over and over. He couldn't even tell which rib was the broken one anymore. They all hurt the same. His whole body was a broken rib.

He sat on the bench and took small breaths infused with the ghosts of cigarettes' past. He wondered if he could even hold a bass guitar right now. There was no way he could sing. It might be months before he could get back to it. He had two shows in the next month, both at shitty bars, but Taylor didn't make a habit of canceling shows. Besides, they were supposed to be warmups with his full band for much bigger events after the EP was unleashed on the world. Not that he had any of that booked yet. The songs were just so good. Taylor expected everything to finally fall into place.

But now he had no tracks and no way to play shows and somehow his dream that had appeared to be solidifying for the briefest of moments was blowing away in a foul wind. Plus, he was scared to go back to his apartment. Gill knew where he lived. Maybe they really would try to cut off his hands. Taylor was always scared of the people he helped committing suicide, but amputation would be a brutal step up.

There was Luisa again. Floating all around him. The reminder of what Taylor's power could really do.

End a life.

They met freshman year, in band. Taylor was playing percussion and laying down bass lines whenever required, and then Luisa walked in halfway through the first semester. Immediate connection. She had this delectable scar on her cheek that caused her to be reserved in public. She was a killer percussionist.

Going against all his hardwired traits, he talked to her and offered to show her around the school. Help her get acclimated. Unspoken was that he was planning to fall deeply in love with her.

At the time, Taylor and his sisters were all trying to understand their powers in different ways. Taylor was late in the knowledge of what he could do, though he always knew it had to do with his hands. They thrummed at night. They wanted to be used.

He knew he made people feel better. His classmates knew it subconsciously too. People wanted to be around him. They wanted to embrace him. They wanted that feeling he supplied without knowing exactly what they were after.

Taylor and Luisa started having sex one week before his dad died. One week before things began to unravel for his family. Junior year would have been impossible without Luisa. They spent all their time together. Then there was the day where she was in the bathroom and he came up behind her and wrapped his arms around her. She was looking in the mirror and she saw it. It wasn't just that sense of well-being that Taylor supplied. He had healed her scar.

"Do it again," she said.

So he did it again. And again. And again. Luisa became obsessed with the way her face looked without the scar. She wanted it to be permanent. That's when Taylor bought the gloves. That's when he began to stop touching other people. That's when he told Luisa it wasn't healthy. They couldn't do it anymore. He wanted to be with her, but they couldn't stand in front of mirrors and watch her scar disappear and reappear.

But their relationship didn't survive. She didn't survive.

A middle-aged woman with a hospital bracelet sat down next to Taylor on the bench and pulled out a cigarette.

"Don't ask, I don't have anymore," she said hoarsely.

"Noted," Taylor said.

Then his phone began buzzing in his pocket.

He figured it was one of his sisters calling to find out where he'd gone. He was surprised to see Gill's number on the screen. There weren't many rings left before it went to voicemail.

"I can't believe you answered," Gill growled.

"Me either," Taylor said.

"You know what else I can't believe?"

"What's that?"

"That my girlfriend was able to beat you up. Musicians, man. Fucking wimps."

"She broke one of my ribs."

Gill laughed for some reason. "Sorry about that. Real sorry. Kacie is too."

"Yeah, sure. You want to pay for my bills?"

"Sure, kid. I'll pay for your bills."

"Seriously?" Taylor said.

"My girl broke your rib. I'll pay. Also want to give you your tracks."

Taylor's heart lurched.

"I made a promise the other night," Gill said. "Want to honor that too. Even though I hate your fucking guts. Your songs are really, really good though. Do something with them."

"I appreciate that."

"Will you heal me again? One more time?"

"No, Gill. I will not."

Gill was silent so long that Taylor figured the deal was off and he'd hung up.

"I respect that," Gill said out of the void. "Also, Kacie thinks you should put the third song first."

"Yes, please. More advice from the woman who kicked my ass would be much appreciated."

"Well, she did have a question. Do you know someone who can fly? She'd love for some lessons."

"I'll meet you at that same bar tomorrow night. Bring the masters. Absolutely do not bring Kacie."

Another growly laugh. "You got it. I'll do one last pass on the mix and I'll recommend a mastering guy."

"Is his girlfriend going to break any of my bones?"

"Musicians, man. Fucking wimps."

3

Phillip felt his body leaning toward this woman next to him with the small hands and the bony chin. He couldn't quite think of her as Mom yet. For now, she was a woman driving a car and Phillip was in the passenger seat and all of his cells were being pulled toward her cells. All the things that bound them together were seeking each other through the space between them. Like seeking like. Hovering and snapping, like the moment before lightning strikes. Phillip's face was so numb he had to reach up with his fingertips to see if it was still there.

The woman moved her arm a little closer, her elbow being offered to him like a microphone. He had lines he'd practiced thousands of times before. Things he thought she should know. Things he wanted her to tell him. But he was afraid that the words would come out wrong; that they would fill the car and choke them both.

"I'm nervous," the woman said. She pulled her arm closer to her, tucking her elbow into her side now. "And I never get nervous. I'm struggling here."

"I'm always nervous," Phillip said.

"This is great news," she said. "Maybe you can give me some pointers."

"Sure."

But then he lapsed into silence again. The pull between them was getting stronger. Overwhelming. Crushing.

"Say you were a mom who had left her child without so much as a goodbye and nary a hello in the intervening years. And you found yourself in a car with him. Your nerves making it hard to think. What would you do?"

She looked at him earnestly, her hands gripping the wheel tighter.

Phillip couldn't meet her gaze. "I would say I'm sorry."

She exhaled, like a cough. Like she'd been punched.

"You're absolutely right," she said.

Phillip felt braver suddenly. She had shifted the power to him. No matter how strange or terrible their situation, his whole life so far without her, he'd been longing for her, and she was here. But how this went was completely up to him. He could end it right now.

"You still haven't said it," he said. Not cruelly.

"I want to," she said. "But it won't come out right. The words aren't strong enough to carry the weight."

He pulled away from her, watched the world shift outside his window.

"So we're just driving?" he says.

"We're just driving." She runs her hand through her hair. "Think of this as the Popemobile. Or Batman's car or something. No bullets can penetrate. No one can see us. We're the only two people in the world."

"Where's Dad?"

"He's going to meet us for dinner."

Phillip felt some small relief. He wasn't sure he could manage this alone.

"I need some more advice. How do I get over these nerves?"

"You could tell me a funny story."

She bit into her lower lip as she thought about it, just like he did when something was on his mind.

"Everyone thinks I'm dead," she said.

Phillip looked at her, half expecting to discover that this whole time she'd been slightly see through. A specter driving a car. It would be easier to understand why she'd completely disappeared from his life if the answer was that she'd died. But by wanting a tidy answer, he was also wishing her into oblivion. It was better if she was here now in all her messiness.

"Why does everyone think you're dead?" he said.

"Not everyone. Just the people I used to know."

He could understand why people would think that. She had pulled off a total disappearance. Not in the way that Mrs. Clark's daughter could disappear. She had taken it much further. She had erased her entire life. Maybe everyone was looking for an explanation. The only way to truly be gone was to die.

"My friend Sammy went to our high school reunion last year. Your dad knows him too. He was a friend of ours." She trailed off for a moment and bit her lip again. Then after coming to an internal decision, she continued. "There was a picture of me in a pamphlet along with three others. 'The Ones We Lost' it said at the top. At the reunion, they all talked about me in hushed tones and only said nice things. And I was never nice, if I'm being honest. Sammy told them about the mistake. Spent the whole night convincing them I was still alive. But I just know. A lot of them liked me better dead."

She turned the car onto the highway and began picking up speed. "Sammy mailed the pamphlet to me. And seeing myself there, it felt real. It felt like I really was dead."

"How did you die?" Phillip said.

"Car accident."

"Maybe they could see the future."

She slowed the car and moved into the right lane. "After that, I would stare in the mirror. To see if I was really there. I would brush my hair more roughly. Pull my belts tighter. Jam my feet into ill-fitting shoes. Just so I could feel my body."

"This story is literally not funny at all," Phillip said.

"What?" She'd loosened up now. He was starting to like her.

"You were going to tell me a funny story."

"Oh right. I didn't get to the funny part yet."

"There's a funny part?"

She smiled. "No. There's no funny part. You called me and I suddenly felt alive again. Like there was someone out there who could actually see me."

Phillip could see her. And he didn't want to stop seeing her.

"Should we go to this dinner with your dad?" she said.

"I don't know," he said.

"Then let's keep driving a little longer."

They moved through town and into the next one. Silent at times. Then talking over each other. The scene outside the window began to look less familiar, and then they were beyond all of Phillip's previous experiences. They kept driving.

Then they were gone.

4

John arrived at the steakhouse thirty minutes early and waited until after the appointed time before he completely lost his shit. The sun was down. The waiter had stopped coming to the table. His heart had stopped beating. His blood had stopped flowing. His nervous system had shut down. Everything that made him human curled in on itself and slumped into the pit of his stomach. He was a husk on a hard chair in the worst steakhouse in town. In the country. John no longer needed to ponder what death's icy embrace would feel like. If he didn't have Phillip, he had nothing. The husk would remain empty forever.

Then his phone rang and his body jolted back to life. His heart slammed in his chest. Blood returned to his extremities. His nervous system whirred. But he was still in the worst steakhouse in the country. And Phillip wasn't with him.

"Hello?" John's voice raked across his dry throat.

"We're okay," Molly said.

His brain screamed at him: *Say something! Say something! Say something!*

Molly took a deep breath. "I thought you should know."

"What are you doing?" John said.

"I don't know."

"Where is he now?"

"He's in the car. I'm picking up food."

John pressed his hand across his forehead, covering his eyes. "What should I do? Should I call the cops?"

"I don't know, John. I don't know what's going on."

"Bring him back. Let's talk."

"Not yet. I can't. Do what you have to do."

She hung up.

Underneath his hand, tears flowed freely, pooling in the spaces between his fingers. The waiter was suddenly there again.

"Want some ice cream?" he said.

"Sure, why not," John said. "To go."

The ice cream was a multicolored puddle in a takeout container by the time John worked up the nerve to approach the police station. The air whooshed around him as he opened the door. He wondered what Phillip was doing now. What he was eating. What they were talking about.

John was once again struck by how quiet the police station was. How little activity seemed to be happening. Then he was confronted with Officer Martins. The same benign face. The same position in his chair behind the counter. John lost his nerve and turned to leave, but then he and Officer Martins were establishing eye contact.

"Did you find your son?" Officer Martins said with a heavy-lidded blink.

"I did," John said. "He was with his teacher. It was out of character for him."

"Kids do the darndest things." He continued to stare at John.

"His mom has him now," John said. Everything that he could possibly say about the situation sounded ridiculous. Paranoid. He could imagine himself making the same face as Officer Martins if their roles were somehow reversed. "He's never met her."

"Is that so?"

"We were supposed to meet for dinner, but they didn't show up."

John watched Officer Martins comprehend where this was going, and it didn't feel good. He felt more foolish than he ever had in his life.

"Are you reporting her for breaking plans?"

John took a step back. "No. Not at all. I just came to tell you that I found my son."

"I will close the books on that case then, sir. Thank you."

"And now he's spending time with his mom."

Officer Martins tilted his head to the side. "Maybe it's for the best."

"Yes, perhaps," John said. But his brain was angry at him again. It demanded to know why John was backing down. Why he was leaving the station. Why he was letting Molly win.

As with Brad Green and his dad and anyone else in authority, John walked away without complaint. He stepped into the heavy night outside the police station and got back into his car and turned on his headlights and tried to see beyond them. John was always looking forward, but he never liked what he saw.

But twenty minutes later when he turned into the driveway, his headlights illuminated Suz huddled on the front porch. She looked as miserable as he felt.

He got out quickly. "Suz? Everything all right?"

"Sorry to show up like this, Mr. Meyer," she said.

"It's okay. You're always welcome here." He looked across the street to her house, but all seemed quiet. He knew that her parents had their troubles. Some very loud fights. It must hard on Suz.

She looked over to the car. "Where's Phillip?"

"I don't know," John said.

"He's with his mom," she said matter-of-factly. As if it was the most obvious thing ever.

"Yes."

"He'll be back."

"I hope so," John said.

"I know you're worried. There's nothing you can do about that. But he won't let you down."

"It's not Phillip I'm worried about."

"I understand," Suz said.

"Are your parents fighting again?" John said.

"Yes."

"You want me to come over and diffuse what I can?"

"No thank you, Mr. Meyer. They'll just get mad at me for sharing our family business. Maybe I can just sit here on the porch for a little while?"

"Do you want to come in? I can get you something to eat."

"If it's okay with you, I'd like to just stay out here alone."

"Of course, Suz. Stay as long as you need."

He walked past her and fought the urge to pat her head. He opened the door and looked back at her slight form. Then he went to the hall closet and pulled out a small blanket from when Phillip was a baby. He returned to the porch and draped it over Suz's shoulders.

She didn't say anything, but she pulled it tighter around her as if it could shield her from the past, the future, and everything in between.

CHAPTER TWELVE

IGNORING THE CRACKS

1

Denise had spent a lot of time in hospitals the last few days. But at least her mom had her own room and a bathroom. Not like she could get up though. Denise stared at her now peaceful mom and tried to banish the vision of her contorted face behind the wheel of the car, her foot still pressed on the gas, her arms thrashing like broken windmills. It had taken all the strength Denise could muster to pull her mom's knee up to get her foot off the accelerator and get the car into park. Add the lady in the car in front screaming the whole time and it was pretty insane. The best was when the ambulance showed up and they thought Denise had been in the accident too. That the only explanation for all that bruising was that she'd been thrown face first into the dashboard.

Her mom had come around for a second before they'd put her into the ambulance. "Don't let Taylor heal me," she'd said but Denise pretended like she hadn't heard it as she followed her to the hospital. And by the time they'd admitted her mom into a room, Denise believed she'd never said it.

That's why it was so infuriating that Taylor was complying with their mom's wishes and he hadn't even been there to hear it.

"I'm telling you, she wouldn't want me to heal her, even for a minute," Taylor said, spread across a wide-mouthed reclining chair that somehow turned into a bed.

"Maybe there are things she'd want to tell us," Denise said. She sat at the edge of her mom's bed and squeezed her foot under the blanket as if her mom needed Denise to hold her in the corporeal realm.

Beth seemed uneasy, perching on the sink across the room and then leaning on the door jamb and then stepping into the hall only to immediately return with a shocked expression, as if surprised to find them all there each time.

"Back me up, Beth," Denise said.

"I can't pretend to know what Mom would want," Beth said, currently in her door jamb position.

"I don't have to pretend," Taylor said.

Denise sighed aggressively. "Let's make a deal. Heal her and let's ask." But Denise knew the first thing her mom would say was how she'd specifically asked for Taylor not to do anything. Denise needed to make it seem like Taylor's idea.

"Say I heal her," Taylor said, finally looking directly at her. "Say that's what she wants. It's not like I can heal her forever. Mom knows that. She's not going to want to be healed for a few minutes and then have to make the decision to go back to the way she was. The way she really is now. She'd want it to play out the way it's meant to. If she wakes up, we'll get a chance to talk to her. Otherwise, we say goodbye in our own ways."

"What's the point of you even having that power if you don't do anything with it." Denise's anger throbbed in her chest, threatening to break her apart.

"What would you have me do, Denise? Give up my whole life to keep my hand on Mom?"

"I would," Denise said.

"I fucking wish you could," Taylor said and slumped lower into the chair. "Then you could stop making me feel like such a failure."

Denise's heart pumped a lump of anger up and out of her chest, and her bruised cheeks ached with the additional heat.

"You ever think how it's funny we all got the wrong powers?" Beth said from the sink, having silently moved at some point during Denise's altercation with Taylor.

"For real," she continued. "Why can't Denise heal Mom? That's like her calling. And I'd give anything to just disappear. And I don't know. Taylor seems like he'd be a badass flyer."

Taylor almost smiled. "I really would."

Denise stood up, suddenly unable to remain still. "I'm sorry, okay. I know I'm the one freaking out here."

"We're all freaking out," Beth said.

"Yeah," Taylor agreed. "You're just the only one taking it out on everyone else."

"I want to talk to Mom again. And that's why I'm aggravated. I'm blaming you for taking away my chance to have a better last conversation with her."

Taylor put his feet on the ground and leaned forward. "I want to tell you something. So you understand. You remember my girlfriend, Luisa?" He cleared his throat. "I did it."

"What?" Denise asked, her body going cold. "She committed suicide..."

Taylor shook his head. "No, I'm not confessing to murder. Holy shit, Denise. Fuck."

Denise sat back down on the bed, once again grabbing her mom's foot under the blanket.

"I healed her," Taylor said. "She had that scar on her cheek from the dog bite when she was a kid."

"I loved that scar," Beth said.

"Me too," Taylor said. "But she didn't."

Taylor's words settled around them. He stared at them, desperate to understand. And then suddenly, Denise did. No wonder Taylor didn't want to use his power or discuss his power or even be around them. He felt responsible for Luisa's death. Now Denise was trying to force him to heal their mother. The things they didn't know about each other could fill a novel.

"Is now a bad time?" a voice called from the door. Denise swung around to find Mr. Scully standing there, skinnier than even the last time she'd seen him. His jacket barely finding a perch on his shoulders.

Denise's tears had managed to find a way out. She needed to blow her nose, but she knew it would hurt too much.

"Oh honey," Mr. Scully said and placed a bunch of flowers on the sink next to Beth. He moved toward Denise. "Were you in the accident too?"

He turned to Beth cradling her arm. "All of you?"

"Not in the accident. We're all just broken," Taylor said, a rasp in his voice. His confession was still raw and damp and hanging in the air. Mr. Scully could surely feel it.

There was regret on Mr. Scully's face now, perhaps he was wishing he hadn't come. Denise reached out and grabbed his shoulder. "I'm happy you're here," she said. "Mom would be glad to see you."

"She looks peaceful," he said.

"I was just thinking the same thing."

Mr. Scully clearly didn't want to move any closer, and Denise could understand that. It was hard to be near a body in rebellion.

"Will you tell her I stopped by?" Mr. Scully said.

Denise patted his arm again. "Of course, we will."

"Thanks for the flowers," Beth said from a new perch on the arm of Taylor's chair. Taylor had leaned forward to rest on her leg and she was rubbing his head.

Mr. Scully turned to leave, and then stopped.

"I was supposed to tell Edna something. A message from one of her students."

Denise's jaw tightened. She knew exactly which student it was going to be.

"His name is Phillip. He wanted me to tell Edna that he had seen her daughter's talent. I'm not sure what he was talking about, but I felt I should pass it along. Does it make any sense to you?"

Denise forced herself to look him directly in the eyes. "I don't have the slightest idea."

"Denise and I have zero talents combined," Beth said.

"Guilty," Denise said.

"It seemed strange to me too," Mr. Scully said. At the doorway, he leaned closer to Denise. "Your mom told me. About what's happening to her. So I know she won't get better. But I truly hope she gets to go home and spend more time with you before she passes."

"Thank you, Mr. Scully," Denise said. "That would mean so much to us. I hope so too."

As soon as the door shut behind him, Beth laughed dryly. "That boy saw you turn invisible, didn't he?"

"Maybe a little," Denise said. "Is that bad? Because when it happened it felt bad, and I don't know why."

"If nobody knows, they can't expect anything from you," Taylor said.

Is that why Denise had never revealed her power to anyone? Or was it that she didn't want to expect more of herself?

"Is he gone?" Her voice was a croak, but it was their mom. Denise ran to the bed, upset that her mom had woken in the brief moment she'd moved away.

"He's gone," Denise said, her voice barely above a whisper.

Taylor winced loudly as he extricated himself from the chair. Beth sidled up next to him. They all stared down at her.

Their mom looked up at each of them in turn. "Hank wanted us to be a thing," she said. "I didn't want it to be awkward."

"I don't think it would have been awkward, Mom," Beth said. "He just wanted to see if you were okay."

"He was probably hoping my boob would pop out from under the sheet."

"He's not some pervert," Denise said. But she looked back to the door, curious if Mr. Scully would be trying to peep in somehow.

"He might be," their mom said. "He watches a ton of porn. Oh, on a side note. When you clear out all my stuff, there's a ton of porn on my computer too."

Taylor stepped back, as if thinking about this new development gave him an electric shock. He bumped into Beth's arm in the sling, and she let out a scream that shredded the air.

Denise couldn't help it. She laughed. And her face felt like it had been split in half again. Taylor put his hands on both of their shoulders, and Denise leaned toward her sister at the same time Beth leaned toward her. They came together at the top of their arms, supporting each other for a moment. It felt really nice.

"I'll be right back," Beth said, and was gone.

2

She needed a cast on her arm. And if Beth could find a doctor to do that, maybe that doctor could put a cast around her heart and lungs and everywhere else that was affected by the sight of her mom in that bed. Beth felt raw and uncontrollable and so very alone. More than anything, she wanted someone to listen to her. To understand her. She wanted someone to tell her it was okay to be sad for herself when her mom was the one dying. She was out of her depth in this current situation, and she desperately needed to flee to somewhere new.

She careened down the hall, past the nurse's station and down the stairs into the lobby of the emergency room. It was quiet. Two elderly ladies stared at a muted television displaying a talk show. Just a close-up of a woman Beth had never seen before, her mouth moving and moving and moving. Like she was calling for help from a parallel dimension.

Beth turned toward the nurse sitting at the counter. He was slumped forward, his chin propped on his open palm.

"I need a cast," Beth said to him.

He looked up at her but kept his head in his hand. "First we'd have to see if it's broken."

"Oh, it's broken. I already had a cast, but I took it off."

"You took it off? Why?"

"I was trying to impress someone."

The nurse sat up straight now, intrigued.

"How long ago did you break it?"

"Yesterday," Beth said.

He looked at her sling.

"Did I impress you, too?" Beth said.

"No."

After she'd filled out her paperwork, Beth moved across the room and sat near the window. She pulled her phone out and flipped it around in her good hand. She turned it on and scrolled to Fran's number. Then she thought better of it and shut it off. Then before she could talk herself out of it again, she went ahead and called Fran.

"She lives," Fran said when she picked up.

A warmth spread across Beth's chest. Relief. Fran sounded like home. Maybe her real home.

"I've been wanting to call," Beth said, her voice carried by a rush of air.

"Was your phone broken?"

"What?" Beth said. She'd never heard Fran's voice like this. Cold. Judgmental.

"I called at least a hundred times. Left a few messages," Fran said. "And you don't have a job anymore, so you definitely had time to call me. Thought maybe the problem was technological."

"No. Just a lot going on in my life."

"A lot? Really?" Fran said. "Because I just got the promotion I've been fighting for, and my girlfriend left me. Fled the scene. Didn't tell anyone where she was going. Though it was obvious she was going home. Running from her problems."

"I didn't mean to run," Beth said, but she knew it was weak.

"I don't think I have a response to that," Fran said.

"Understandable. You shouldn't. It was a dumb thing to say. Of course, I meant to run. What I wanted to say was that I didn't mean to give into myself again."

"You're the most terrified person I have ever met."

Fran's statement scratched at her like a feral cat. Beth had never thought of herself as scared. She was strong. Capable. Steely. The running was to protect those around her from shrapnel as Beth plowed her way through barriers.

"My mom is dying," Beth said. "She's in the hospital now. And I had an altercation with an old friend and my arm is broken and I'm in pain. All over. I'm wounded, Fran."

"I see what this is," Fran said, her voice becoming increasingly clipped. "You need me again. Your home life is in shambles and you're looking for another place to flee. When you didn't like how things were going here, you ran as fast as you could away from me, and now you want to run double that speed back."

"Can I?" Beth said. "I'm sorry. About everything. Let me come back. I need to come back."

Fran hung up.

"Beth Clark," a voice called from the door leading into the emergency room.

Beth stared up at the nurse, unable to decide what she should do next.

"Beth Clark."

Let them keep calling her. Let them move on to the next person. Let them forget about her.

She held her phone out in front of her. Waiting. Waiting.

Waiting.

3

Her mom was asleep again, and Denise found herself once more at the foot of the bed. Taylor looked pale in his chair, his arms clasped loosely in front of him.

"You think that nurse would give me morphine?" Taylor said suddenly. They hadn't spoken in at least half an hour. After their argument earlier, Denise had been scared to return to the previous conversation. "I think she's kind of into me."

Denise shook her head. "Not 'lose her job' into you."

"My rib hurts so bad."

"I wish I could do something for you."

Taylor smiled. "I know you do. Trust me. I know you do." He shifted in the chair and grunted. "I'm not mad at you, by the way."

"I'm not mad at you, either," Denise said.

"Glad we sorted that out."

"Me too."

Denise's phone buzzed in her pocket. Unknown number.

"Hello?" she said.

"I can't believe you gave me your real number."

"I surprised myself."

John made a whimpering noise.

"Did you get a dog?" Denise said. She glanced over at Taylor, but he seemed to have nodded off. She got up and left the room.

"I can't control the noises coming out of me," John said.

The hallway floors gleamed under Denise's feet as she moved slowly away from her mom's room. Twisting through turn after turn. Slowly losing her place.

"It's my son," John said. "He's gone."

"Phillip? What happened?"

"His mom took him. I don't know where they are."

"We'll find him," Denise said. "We'll find him."

"How?" John said, loudly weeping now.

"We'll figure something out."

"Thank you for picking up my call. I don't have anyone to turn to. I don't have any friends."

Denise leaned against the wall past a silver elevator door. "I don't have any friends either," she said.

"Do you want to come over?" John said.

Denise thought of her mom sleeping peacefully in the hospital bed. Her brother moaning through a night of pain on an uncomfortable chair. Her sister probably halfway out of town by now. It felt good to have a place to go. A place where she was needed. "I do," she said. "Very much so. I'm on my way now."

She hit the down button for the elevator and was anxious to see where it would take her.

Day Three

NOT A MOMENT TO LOSE!

CHAPTER THIRTEEN

REFUSING TO BUDGE

1

Denise's phone buzzed lightly somewhere across the room. She rolled out from under John's arm, careful not to bang her face on his bony elbow, and slid to the end of the bed. Pale phone light glowed from her purse on the dresser. She grabbed it and stepped into the hallway. The door to Phillip's empty room stood open as if in shock.

"Hello?" Denise said as she tiptoed into the dark front room.

Beth made a surprised sound on the other end of the phone. "I didn't think you'd answer."

"I always answer," Denise said. She sat down in a tattered brown chair.

"This time, the food ate me."

"God. That's horrible."

Beth exhaled. "It was a rabid pack of Starburst. They were all over me like ants."

"Brutal." The early part of the night began trickling back. Before John called about Phillip. Before Denise had driven to his house and clutched him like he might be sucked into the stratosphere. Before John had finally fallen asleep, exhausted from worry. Before this phone call with Beth. "Where are you?"

"I'm at the hospital," Beth said. "A better question is where are you?"

"You went back?"

"You sound surprised."

"I thought you'd fled the scene," Denise said.

"Let's just say I tried. But only you were successful."

Denise curled into the chair, her knees up against her chest. "It's a long story."

"I'm sure. But don't worry. Mom didn't wake up and overshare again."

"How is Taylor?"

"He's in serious pain. Moaning in his sleep. Did you know any of that about Luisa?"

"No," Denise said. "We are terrible siblings."

"We didn't grow apart," Beth said. "We are apart. If we want to be closer, we have to work at it."

"That's what I want."

"I think I do too. But please don't tell me about your porn preferences." Beth laughed, though she sounded stern. Serious.

"What kind of porn do you think Mom watches?" Denise shivered. She made a promise to herself that she was never going to look on that computer.

"Fully clothed," Beth said. "They just quote Jane Austen to each other."

"Do they climax?"

"Yes, but silently. Into their knickers."

"What about the O-Face?"

"More of a bemused smirk," Beth said.

Lodged between two seemingly unfixable situations, a dying mother and a missing boy, it felt good to laugh. "One could be called Mansfield Pork."

"Scent and Flexibility."

"North-Banger Abbey."

"Cumma."

"I'm hanging up," Denise said.

"Wait," Beth said in a rush. "When are you coming back? I need you here."

"Soon," Denise said. "I promise. I just have something to take care of."

"You mean someone," Beth said.

Maybe Beth did know her more than she thought. "I'm glad you didn't leave."

"I didn't have a single food dream when we slept in the same bed last night. You're the best sleep aid on the market."

"Tonight then," Denise said. "Tonight I'll chase your dreams away."

"Mansfield Pork was the worst one," Beth said.

"Now I'm really hanging up," Denise said, but she waited, listening to the comforting sound of Beth's slow, steady breathing.

2

A light had flashed outside the window all through the night, letting travelers know that there were still vacancies if they liked rooms that smelled like stale cigarettes, incontinent dogs, and black mold. The woman who hoped to become his mom had bought them cheeseburgers and milkshakes before stopping at the motel. Phillip knew they had gone too far. In miles for sure; he had no idea where they were. But they'd also gone too far in the ruse. They weren't a mother and son on a small vacation. They were running from their previously established life and by the time the woman had fallen asleep on the uncomfortable bed, they both knew they'd made an enormous mistake.

Phillip's heart had pulsed angrily all night, matching the silent warning of the light outside the window. As the sun poked in through a crack in the door, Phillip got up from his side of the bed, the gulf that had separated him from the woman was filled with pillows. He crossed to her bag and with a glance to make sure she was still asleep, he pulled out her phone.

He pushed the button on the side and a number pad appeared on the screen, waiting for a passcode. Phillip tried his birthday, just in case, but that didn't work. Then he remembered that his dad used his face to open his phone. Maybe this woman's would be the same.

He crept closer, her face serene and unlined in the pale morning light. Phillip held the phone directly in front of her and the phone switched to the home screen. He scurried to the bathroom and shut the door. Only one bulb worked, and it flickered like the beginning of a movie. He pressed the phone icon and then, with a rush, remembered he still didn't know his dad's number.

The thing about his dad was that he was always there. Always. Phillip never had to wonder. He felt a rush of love so pure and so strong that he almost fell over. Tears filled his eyes with big plans to rush down his face. How could he leave his dad when his dad would never, ever leave him?

Phillip navigated to the woman's contacts hoping to see his dad's name. Nothing. She must have him under a fake name or something. Like his dad did for her. He scrolled and scrolled. Name after name of perfect strangers. Then it was there. Sammy. The guy his mom had told him about. The one that had been friends with his dad too. He hit the call button.

It rang. And rang. And rang. Then an automated voicemail. Phillip hung up. He tried again. The ringing and then the voicemail. Again. And again. He couldn't reach Sammy.

Then he thought of Suz. And how when she'd started seventh grade, her parents had given her a phone. Another thing that had set them apart, so Phillip had never called her on it. But he could remember vividly the day she got it. How she kept singing her new number. "Doesn't it sound like a commercial jingle?" It was a repetition of fives and nines and if Phillip concentrated, he could still hear her singing it. He could see her mouth forming the numbers.

He dialed.

Suz picked up on the second ring.

"It's me," Phillip said.

"Phillip? Where are you? Your dad is freaking out. Also, I waited on your porch for the longest time last night hoping you'd come home. My parents had probably the worst fight ever. I thought they were going to kill each other. Like at the exact same time. Like lunge for each other's jugulars with the butter knives with the gold handles in perfect synchronization. Then their blood shooting out and mixing together in a way they would definitely hate."

"Suz, hold on a second. I need to tell you something," Phillip said, finally able to catch a break in her rambling.

"Why do you sound so creepy?"

"I think my mom kidnapped me. By accident."

"By accident?"

Phillip listened through the door to hear if she was moving around yet. "Yeah. We just drove away. But since I can't get back on my own, it feels kind of like kidnapping. But more pleasant."

"I'm not going to tell your dad you said that," Suz said. "He's seriously losing it. Oh, but that lady came over again. She's kind of hot, huh? I wish she'd come to my house."

"Suz, for real. What am I supposed to do?"

"Call the cops."

"But I don't want her to get in trouble."

Suz paused for a moment. "Tell her you want to go home then."

Phillip nodded vigorously even though Suz couldn't see him. "That's a really good idea."

"Thanks. I'm fucking brilliant. Come home soon because I have a ton of stuff to tell you."

"I have so much to tell you too," Phillip said.

"I'm sorry I held that guy's hand."

Phillip's heart exploded and blood rushed to every major artery at once. And then another call came through. It was Sammy.

"I have to answer this call," Phillip said.

"Get un-kidnapped soon," Suz said and hung up.

He wished more than anything he could keep talking to Suz. Whatever came next could never compare to Suz apologizing for the hand holding.

"Sammy?" Phillip said.

"Molly? No, that's not Molly." Sammy had a pleasant voice. He beamed kindness across the country to this dank motel. "You must be Phillip. I think Molly was trying to call me."

"It was me."

"Did she tell you?" Sammy said, a notch of excitement in his voice.

"What?"

"We're getting married. Well, I asked her. Before she left. But no answer yet. Is she wearing the ring?"

Phillip thought about the woman's hands on the steering wheel. There wasn't a single ring. Not even an indent where one used to be.

"That's quite the pause," Sammy said. "It's okay. I'm guessing she didn't tell you either, did she?"

"No," Phillip said.

Sammy inhaled sharply. "Has something happened?"

"Kind of," Phillip said.

"Is Molly hurt?"

"No. Nobody is hurt." The tears were there again. Phillip knew he had to tell Sammy, but he felt this overwhelming sense of duplicity. He wanted to stand by the woman. The woman who had abandoned them. The woman who was still his mom. The woman who was his mom. His mom. He wanted to stand by his mom.

"Is Molly there?"

"Yes, she's asleep. We're at a motel."

"What happened?"

"We drove away. We drove away from everybody. We drove away from my dad. I need to tell him where I am. I need him to come get me."

Phillip told him the name of the motel and the name of the restaurant where they'd gotten cheeseburgers.

"Phillip, you in there?" Molly's voice was hoarse outside the bathroom door. She sounded terrified.

3

The best way to pretend everything was okay was to buy Pop Tarts. That's why Beth was in front of the Jewel first thing in the morning yet again, sitting in her car watching people zombie-shuffle into the grocery store. Nobody walked in pairs this early in the morning. Every single shopper was alone. Mornings were for the lonely.

But why had Beth parked in a spot that offered the best view of the entire front of the store? Why hadn't she gotten out yet to procure her breakfast pastry? Why was she gripping the steering wheel like she was about to tumble over a cliff?

Well, it was because of the short woman who was at that moment walking with confident purpose toward the sliding doors of the Jewel. The very same girl who Beth had yesterday been worried she'd never talk to again, and now she felt an uncontrollable urge to avoid. Beth had her new cast and her sling and the knowledge of her mom's porn stash as well as her impending death and Beth hadn't showered or changed clothes or brushed her teeth and now seemed like a bad time to figure out what Renata meant to say after "I think maybe." This wasn't the moment for full disclosures.

Then the sliding doors whipped open again and there was Renata, striding confidently toward Beth's car. Startled, Beth reached for her keys and dropped them on the floor. Then she banged her broken arm on the gear shift and when she looked up, Renata was standing outside her window.

Beth opened the door but remained in the car. Renata leaned down to her.

"I did the same thing," she said with a tight smile.

"What do you mean?" Beth said.

"I came here today at the same time hoping you'd be here."

"I doubt that."

"Is it so hard to believe that someone would come here specifically for you?"

"I guess not," Beth said. "I'm cool as hell."

"You are cool. I always thought that. Still do."

Renata indicated towards the shining new cast that Beth wore on her arm.

Beth couldn't help it. She blushed so hard that she thought her eyeballs might explode.

Renata stood up straight. "You know the nicest thing that anyone has ever done for me?"

Beth shook her head.

"Pretended that I hadn't broken her arm to protect my feelings."

"You didn't break my arm, Renata. I broke my arm by falling down the stairs. Like an asshole."

"Was your brother moving it around for you, somehow? Didn't it hurt like hell?"

"You know the nicest thing anyone has ever done for me?" Beth said.

"It's definitely not break your arm."

"When you climbed into my car to get rid of that bee for me. That was the moment."

"I'd do it again," Renata said.

Beth instinctively looked to the back windshield. "I hope you never have to."

Renata squatted next to the car and reached onto the floorboard and grabbed the keys that had fallen. She placed them flat on her palm and lifted them up to Beth.

"I always liked you," Renata said. "I wanted you to notice me when we were kids. I wanted to be your friend so bad."

"I was a bitch back then," Beth said. "Still am."

"A badass bitch."

Beth had thought she was done blushing, but apparently she had never-ending supply of embarrassment.

"But you aren't gay, are you?" Beth said.

"Not even a little."

"That's really too bad. I just broke up with my girlfriend because I'm selfish and it's the perfect time for someone to swoop in and try to change me."

"I can help with the changing part," Renata said.

"You still want to be my friend? Even though I have the hots for you?"

Now suddenly Renata was blushing.

"I'm flattered, actually."

Beth thought about that. Flattering someone with her specific adoration.

"If you can get me to stop thinking about Pop Tarts and dreaming about talking food."

"It's so crazy you said that," Renata said. "I've had this idea for years of doing workout videos and the whole time I'm getting heckled by talking food."

"Yes, I'm in."

"What?"

Beth smiled. "I thought you were asking me to help you produce it."

"I guess I was," Renata said. "Hey, can I sign your cast?"

Renata reached into the car and took Beth's broken arm. She slowly pulled it out of the sling, holding the weight of Beth's arm in her hands. She looked up at Beth and smiled. Then she hunched over the cast and began writing.

When she was done, she stood and backed away. Beth looked down to find a perfect cartoon bee with shaded dark stripes and shimmery wings and curlicued antennae. It was also grinning maniacally.

"Changed my mind," Beth said. "This is the nicest thing anyone has done for me."

CHAPTER FOURTEEN

COMPROMISING ON NOTHING

1

Edna was back in her bedroom. The room was warm, stuffy with the remembrance of movie lights and bodies and expectant breaths. But she was alone now. She was safe. The sheets felt cool and crisp under her. She arched her back and let her hair fall onto the pillow. There was no pain. No resistance. Her body was back on her team.

The door opened and a puff of air cascaded over her arms and chest. She sat up and there was Nolan, still in his handyman outfit. But he was no longer smirking. He looked calm and refreshed. Like he had on Sunday mornings when he'd slept in and Edna had made him pancakes and sausage.

"You're still in your handyman outfit," Edna said.

Nolan smiled. "So are you."

Edna looked down to find that she was also wearing khaki pants and a white t-shirt and a belt loaded with tools.

"What were you fixing?" Nolan said.

"Nothing. Not a single thing."

"Take it off."

Edna reached down to undo the belt, but it was stuck. She yanked and yanked and yanked but it wouldn't budge.

"Let me," Nolan said, and sat on the bed. He gingerly reached over and undid the latch. The belt fell with a thump onto the bed.

"I miss you," Edna said.

"I miss you too." He smiled. He was so close to her. He was exactly as she remembered.

"Is that really you?"

Nolan shrugged. "I think so."

"So am I dead?"

"Not yet." But he stared at her, as if he was a little unsure.

Edna moved toward him, her hand reaching for his, but he pulled away, rising to his feet.

"I need to know, Nolan," she said. "Is there an afterlife? Will I see you again?"

He smiled once more. "I don't want to ruin the surprise."

And then she was awake, gasping for breath in her hospital bed. A machine beeped pleasantly next to her. Taylor huddled under two blankets on the horrific couch-chair thing in the corner.

Edna closed her eyes again and searched her head for any sign of the tumor laughing at her. But it had been silent since the car accident.

"Nolan," Edna said because she liked hearing his name. She could still feel his weight on the mattress next to her. A dissipating relic from the dream.

The sun peeked through the slats of the window. Edna wondered how many days had passed. She felt curiously well. Like she'd slept away her glioblastoma. Perhaps she was waking from a coma. Or maybe she'd dreamed the whole tumor thing. But when she tried to get up, she felt the dizziness and the ache behind her eyes, and she knew it was all true. She was on her way out.

"Taylor," she said. He didn't move. "Taylor!"

He snorted in his sleep and then groaned. His broken rib was clearly bothering him. He could barely extricate himself from the blankets.

"You up, Mom?" he said. "Sorry. I fell asleep."

"You think I'm trying to fix everyone? I keep having these handyman dreams. It's hard to explain."

"You're the handyman?" Taylor said.

"Sure."

Taylor peered at her. It was unnerving. It was the same look Nolan had given her when he thought she wasn't looking. It was just as inscrutable coming from Taylor.

"I wouldn't call it fixing, necessarily," Taylor finally said, and alleviated some tension in the room. "I would call it changing. After Dad died, you wanted us to fill the void. And when we couldn't, you gave up on us."

Slapping him seemed like a good idea, but it would require too much energy. Instead, Edna sighed very loudly.

"Not what you wanted to hear?" Taylor said.

"That's not how I would interpret the dream at all."

"You know, Beth has been having vivid dreams too. About talking food."

"Well, that's easy," Edna said. "She gained at least twenty pounds. Mine is more nuanced. There's a meaning there trying to come through."

"I think we should stop talking about dreams," Taylor said.

Some of the anger Edna had felt before the car accident and her subsequent deposit into the hospital was creeping back. Was she angry at Taylor for not being more like Nolan? Had she always been a little angry at him? He didn't even really look like Nolan. He took after Edna in almost everything.

"Okay, so maybe I did want you to change," Edna said.

"A lot of people have wanted me to do that."

"Specifically, I thought you were kind of weak. I wanted to toughen you up."

"Compared to Dad? The guy was literally the strongest man that ever lived."

Edna could see Nolan's hands now. Creased and calloused from manual labor. Perfect moon-shaped nails. Palms as big as potholders.

"When I realized what he could do, oh my," Edna said. "He could pull a tree out of the ground and yank up all the roots. I was ready to have thousands of his babies."

"Gross, Mom."

"I say it because I want you to feel it too, one day. You need to feel that true love. When your dad died, he grabbed as much of me as he could with his enormous hands and took it all with him. I was hollowed out. And it never filled in. The shell just cracked instead."

"Hard to believe that a bee took him out. Stupid things are so slow and stupid and stupidly slow."

"Do you blame me?" Edna said, veering into new territory with her youngest child.

"Did you lock him out?" Taylor said.

"He could have pulled the door from its hinges. He could have crashed through a wall. He could have pulled off the roof. I couldn't lock your father out. Not for real."

"How about symbolically?"

"Yeah, I locked the door. I was mad at him."

"About what?"

This was why she never talked about it. This was why she pushed everyone away. This was why she couldn't make things right, not ever. "I don't know, Taylor. Do you understand? I don't know why I was so mad at him. I don't know why I locked him out. Some inconsequential bullshit, a five-minute flare-up, and then I never got to see him again. And there you all were staring at me like I had answers. Or like I'd killed him on purpose."

"So instead of breaking down the door, he sat on the porch and a bee stung him and his throat closed up, and that was it."

"That was it."

"I don't blame you."

"Beth does."

"She just hates herself and takes it out on everyone else."

Edna felt a sudden sadness for her oldest daughter. A desire to pull her close. To stroke her hair. But she wasn't a little girl anymore. She was a fully grown, fucked up adult who probably didn't want her mom to hug her anymore. When was the last time they had hugged? Was there ever a time?

"You can't fix us, Mom," Taylor said. "So there's no need to have the handyman dream anymore."

"I wonder what I would do if I'd been the one with a superpower."

"You'd find a completely different way to screw it up."

Edna laughed.

Taylor bowed his head. "I know Dad would be disappointed in me. I let a man control my future while my power made me even weaker. And his girlfriend broke my rib by kicking me when I was down. Literally. Hundred percent he'd be disappointed."

Edna had never really thought about if she'd wanted a power. But the weight of it was dragging her children down, dragging them down along with the expectations they placed on themselves, and the ones they imagined from their dead, amazing father.

"Not everyone is destined for greatness."

"I'm not even destined for mediocrity," Taylor said.

"It's funny to get to the end of your life and try to find meaning," Edna said.

"Yeah. Sounds truly hilarious."

"I have motherly advice for you."

"Lay it on me." Taylor shifted on the chair and groaned with pain.

"There's no meaning to anything," Edna said. "You're beating yourself up and holding yourself to this high standard and you're making yourself miserable. Do whatever you like to do. If you don't like something, give it up. At the end of your life, what gnaws at you are the times you chose to go against your own happiness. When you thought something was important and took yourself out of the equation. You can't go back, Taylor. You only go forward. Until you can't anymore."

"I don't want you to die, Mom. Not yet."

"You and me both."

The door opened and Beth stomped into the room with a box of Pop Tarts. Someone had drawn a rather cute bee on her cast.

Edna didn't have a clue what advice to give Beth.

"I'm giving you the house, Beth," she said. "You need to settle down."

2

Denise had tried to leave John behind. When he'd gotten the call from some guy named Sammy with a lead on where Phillip might be, he'd gone into shock at the foot of the bed. Denise had stood up and grabbed her purse, convinced that if she had Beth and Taylor with her, they could bring that boy home.

But John hadn't let her go alone. It was hard to explain to someone with a missing child that he needed to just wait at home for someone else to take care of it.

"I don't understand," John said as Denise pulled the car into the hospital parking lot. "Why do we need your brother and sister?"

That word need bounced around the car with its sharp edges and hard metal center. But retrieving Phillip felt like a rescue mission. Like something big and important and heroic. Denise didn't feel up to the challenge. She was worried she'd bungle the whole thing, and John would never see Phillip again. Denise knew what she was capable of, and she knew what Beth and Taylor were capable of and if they assembled that power, they could save anyone.

Except their mom.

"Stay here," Denise said and got out before John could respond. She left the car running along the curb at the end of the emergency room awning.

She felt the exhilaration from when she'd first started going on patrol. That tingling sensation, as if all of her nerve endings were quivering with excitement, or fear, or maybe a mix of both. But this time, there was a purpose. An achievable goal. A way to really do something good.

The sliding doors opened with a whoosh and Denise ambled past a nurse pushing an elderly woman in a wheelchair. She hurried into the stairwell and sprinted up the stairs two at a time. She was at the fourth floor before she realized that she'd been invisible the whole time. She forced herself to return to sight and barreled into the hallway and toward her mom's room.

The door was slightly ajar, and Denise flung it open, ready to compel her siblings to join her, but there was a nurse leaning over her mom attempting to fix her sheets.

Taylor was in his spot on the chair eating a Pop Tart. Beth was nowhere to be found.

"Heard you found a comfortable bed to sleep in last night," Taylor said.

"That's not why I left," Denise said as her adrenaline plummeted.

"So you're denying it?"

"No, I did sleep in a great bed."

Denise looked over at her mom, but it was hard to tell if she was asleep or not. She could easily be faking so she didn't have to talk to the nurse.

"I need your help," Denise said as the nurse moved over to a chart and began writing something down.

"Need me to make the bed for you?" Taylor said. "Fluff your pillow?"

"You're not some martyr because you slept on an uncomfortable chair," Denise said.

The nurse threw an indiscriminate smile into the room, not necessarily meant for anyone, or maybe meant for everyone, and then she left.

"Where's Beth?" Denise said.

"She went to find a bathroom outside the room so I'm assuming she's taking a dump."

"Lovely," Denise said. She thought of John in the car, counting the minutes and all the ways that Phillip could be getting further and further away from the hotel where he'd stayed the night. Why had she left the car running? If John felt frantic enough, she wouldn't put it past him to drive away without her. That's what she would do. Her heart lurched from side to side and Denise had to grab the wall for support.

"Steady there," Taylor said. He hoisted himself to his feet. "You look like you're going to pass out. But I'd recommend against it, because I can't catch you." He gestured to the chair. "Sit."

Denise staggered to the chair and sat in the residual warmth from Taylor's body still ensconced in the hospital blankets. She glanced at her mom, but her eyes were still closed.

"What's going on?"

"I'm sorry about what happened," Denise said. "I had no idea. About your girlfriend."

"It's not like I told you," Taylor said. "It's okay. We're okay."

Denise sniffled. "I want us to do something together. Something important."

"Is this some kind of trust fall shit?"

"No," Denise said. "I want to save a boy."

Their mom lurched awake, her voice raspy with sleep. "Is it Phillip?"

"Yes," Denise said. "He's not in any danger I don't think. But he's been kidnapped. By his mom. Who he's never met."

"Sounds like a soap opera," Taylor said. "I think you can handle it."

The door opened and Beth stood there with two cans of pop. "Handle what?" she said.

"Oh, Denise wants to go on a rescue mission. She's trying to recruit us like we're The Avengers or something."

"I think we're more like the Justice League," Beth said. "You need my help?"

Denise had never been more grateful for her sister before. "Please," she said.

"I'll stay here and look after mom," Taylor said.

Their mom scoffed. "If you think I want you here staring at me, you're fucking mistaken. Stop arguing and go with your sister before I get up and break another one of your ribs."

"I guess that settles that," Beth said.

"A guy in a wheelchair might stop by," Taylor said, which Denise know understood as the reason he didn't want to come along at first. "Hopefully his girlfriend doesn't start kicking you."

"The masters?" Denise said.

Taylor shrugged. "We'll see."

Denise got up from the chair, the past wooziness gone. "We have to go. I'll explain everything on the way."

"We don't have to talk like superheroes the whole time, do we?" Taylor asked.

"There's not a moment to lose!" Denise said as she disappeared from sight. She ran down the hallway alone, but she knew they were both following her.

3

Just because Denise was hot didn't mean she could solve any situation. John felt like a damn fool sitting in the passenger seat of her car in front of a hospital when Phillip could be leaving that hotel for unknown locales. John needed to take the information he was given and strike. He needed Phillip back.

But then there was the other part of him. The part that thought maybe Denise did know what she was doing. Maybe the only way they could get Phillip back was by doing it in this exact way. He had to be sitting in front of this hospital right now. Denise had to be getting her brother and sister. And this was all happening while Denise's mom was dying.

Finally, after years of doing everything alone, John had a partner. He'd only known Denise for two days, but it was the least alone he'd felt in years. As he sat in the car watching the sliding doors of the emergency room open and close, he realized he was desperately in love, although he'd only seen Denise three times in his whole shitty life. If this separation counted, while he sat alone contemplating his misaligned heart, then when she returned that would be the fourth time he'd seen her and he wanted there to be so many more.

He wanted to rescue Phillip. And he wanted to believe Denise could help. So he didn't jump into the driver seat and drive away. He just stared at those doors. Waiting. Tensing his muscles. Willing Phillip to stay put. Stay put until they could get there. Until John could bring him home.

Then suddenly, there she was. Somehow radiating a light with the sun beating down. Her bandaged face glowing. He squeezed his thighs and leaned forward to the dashboard.

Denise got into the driver's seat while Beth and Taylor got into the back. All three of them looked wrecked. Pale and hurting.

But then Taylor reached across the seat and put his hand on John's shoulder. A cascade of certainty crashed against him. They were going to pull this off. They were going to get Phillip. The tears were gone. The fear was gone.

"We got this, man," Taylor said. "We got this."

And then they were off.

CHAPTER FIFTEEN

COMMANDEERING THE FUTURE

1

Phillip stared at the woman. At his mom. He could see himself in that face. She stared back at him. She could probably see herself in his face. If neither of them moved, it was like some kind of warped mirror that transmorphed their expressions. Phillip was trying to look relaxed, but she looked worried.

They sat at a table in the lobby of the motel. Someone had put out donuts and small containers of yogurt and little boxes of cereal and she had said "This is nice" a few times as if it were a magic phrase that could turn the table of food into something that was actually tasty.

Phillip hadn't eaten yet because he was stalling. That's what Sammy had told him to do. Stall. Sammy was going to call his dad who was then going to drive here and pick him up. A little twist of sadness curled somewhere in his ribcage. He wanted to get to know her. His mom. But not like this.

"Aren't you hungry?" she said.

"Yes," he said. He didn't want to lie to her.

"You don't like cereal?"

"I love cereal."

"Me too."

But Phillip noticed she wasn't eating either. Maybe she was stalling too.

"Can I tell you something?" she said.

He nodded.

"It's been so great meeting you."

He smiled because he agreed very, very much.

"But I have no idea what to do next," she said.

"Me either," Phillip said. He almost told her that his dad was coming but he thought she might get spooked. It was better to wait this one out.

"I don't think we should go to LA. Not yet."

"Okay."

"You like road trips?" she said.

"I've never been on one. This is the furthest I've ever been from home."

She nodded vigorously. "It's settled then. We're going on a road trip."

"To where?" Phillip said.

"Everywhere." She stuffed the small boxes of cereal into her purse and grabbed two donuts. "We better stock up."

"We're leaving already?"

With a purpose now, she was vibrating with energy. "The road calls."

Phillip was terrible at stalling.

"Before we leave," he said. "Can we go to a real restaurant? Get some real food?"

"That's a fine idea, Phillip."

"Thanks, Mom," he said, just to try it out.

2

Taylor didn't have to look up to know that John had tossed him another glance from the front seat. That dude was jonesing for something he couldn't understand. Taylor had given John a little boost of confidence as he'd gotten into the car, and it had changed everything about his demeanor. When Taylor had let go, John hadn't come all the way back down. He'd held on to some of that good feeling. Taylor had never seen anything like it. Most people got sad after Taylor let go, they wanted that sense of well-being for free, with no work on their part. John, on the other hand, was willing to fight for it. Also, he seemed to have figured Taylor was involved somehow, and he kept glancing over with question marks in his eyes.

This was playing out while he was trying to find his kid as well. Taylor found him impressive. So far, he liked this John guy. Taylor was even experiencing a bit of the thrill that Denise wanted them to feel. The idea of helping John find his kid, that the three of them might be called upon to use their powers, was exhilarating. Taylor had spent so much of his life hiding what he could do, it was pretty awesome to think there might be a greater purpose to his power. He wasn't about to get carried away, though. Instead, he and Beth had been shit talking in the backseat while Denise drove them toward the last known whereabouts of the kid. Some motel about an hour-and-a-half away.

Beth nudged him in the arm and pointed at Denise and John's intertwined fingers, gripping each other hard, as if they were afraid one of them might fall out of the car. "If they weren't saving Phillip, they would most likely be using this time to plan their wedding."

Taylor agreed. There was definitely something there between these two. Hard to believe they'd just met. Other than the looks John had thrown him, it was almost as if Taylor and Beth weren't there. Denise was soothing him, trying to take his mind off of things during the drive. They had formed a soft warm bubble around themselves.

Then Taylor figured out the perfect way to explain it. "Did you know we were going to have to watch their auras fuck the whole time?"

"My aura has already vomited three times," Beth said.

"Mine got a vasectomy," Taylor said and they both looked up to the front seat at the same time expecting to share a laugh. Then Taylor felt it and he knew Beth did too, a little something akin to jealousy that wiped the smile from both of their faces. Taylor's aura was lonely. Beth's probably was too.

"The thing to keep in mind," Denise was saying in the front seat, "is that they didn't get very far. Maybe she had second thoughts or doubled back. Or they just drove in circles."

"I don't think this was planned out," John said. "I can't imagine she came into town to kidnap Phillip. Things got out of hand at some point, and she's probably freaking out right now."

"Very charitable of you, John," Beth said. "But she still has Phillip. And clearly her plan changed at some point. So we'll do what we have to do to get him back."

Apparently, Beth was feeling that surge of feeling about the upcoming rescue as well. Taylor tried to meet her eye, but she was in superhero mode. Her shoulders back, her chin thrust up.

"Yes," Taylor said. "Whatever it takes."

"I'm so grateful to all of you," John said, and Taylor was amazed at his certainty in their abilities even though he didn't know what any of them could actually do.

Denise somehow squeezed his hand tighter, and Taylor watched to see if his fingers might pop off like Play-Doh.

Beth turned, her shoulders still squared. "I think I see the sign for the motel up there," she said in her clipped superhero voice.

Taylor turned slowly so as not to send a spasm of pain from his ribs across his entire body, and he saw it too. He couldn't help it. His heart rate spiked. This whole rescue thing was exciting.

John swung his head around, tracking a car as it moved past them in the opposite direction. "That was them!" he said.

Denise slammed the brakes.

"What the fuck?" Taylor could barely force the words out. He clenched his teeth and cradled his arms across his abdomen. A burning sensation tore through his chest.

But nobody cared.

The car behind them honked loudly because they were now blocking the flow of traffic. Denise inched forward and turned on her left turn signal.

"Turn around!" John said while clutching the back of his seat, his body now facing the rear window as he watched his son moving away from them.

Taylor had never seen true anguish like that. Like his chest pain was being reenacted in John's expression. Next to him, Beth's body involuntarily lifted off the seat as if she could fly through the roof of the car. Taylor put his gloved hand on her shoulder and pushed her back into her seat.

Denise finally managed to make a left into a gas station. She whipped the car around 180 degrees a little too quickly. Then they were back on the street in hot pursuit of Philip and his mother.

"Can I go over the speed limit?" Denise said.

"Yes!" Beth said.

Taylor tucked himself against the door, bracing himself for future maneuvers that were above Denise's pay grade.

"Please go faster," John said quietly. "I don't see them anymore."

Denise slowly pressed the gas and they crept to a higher speed.

"Anyone see them?" John said.

Taylor looked down the side streets as they passed. A couple of busier intersections. The adrenaline that had spiked as they neared the motel had sprung a leak. The more they looked for the other car, the easier it was to feel that they'd missed their only chance.

Beth tightened next to him. "Speed up," she urged Denise. "I think I see them."

Now, with the rescue moments ahead of them, Taylor began cursing his broken rib. It was a painful tie to his life before this moment. A reminder that he rarely made good decisions. He was going to change that.

John strained forward. "You think that's them?"

The car jumped forward, and Taylor winced again.

They didn't seem to be getting any closer. The light ahead of them changed red and the other car was far past it.

"What do I do?" Denise said.

"Don't stop," Taylor said. "You got this."

Beth looked over at Taylor and he shrugged. He could talk like a superhero too.

"You have to stop, Denise," John said. He tapped her hand.

She thought for a moment and then she slammed on the brakes, screeching to a stop just before the intersection and the red light.

They all looked at each other, nobody daring to say what they all knew. They were never going to catch them.

Beth pushed open her door and hopped out. They all watched her run toward the intersection, a stillness in the car. The weight of possibility. Would she really do it? Then Beth leapt into the air, tucking her arms along her side, and hurtled after the car that might possibly contain John's son.

3

John's vision was swarmed by flashing lights, as if a parade had assembled to bolster the sight of Beth achieving his childhood dream of flight. He was glad he was sitting or he would have fallen over. He arched over the dashboard to look up into the sky, convinced that he would see nothing. That he had imagined it.

But there she was, defying gravity. Arching her back like a cat as she flew through the air after Molly and Phillip.

As he'd suspected the whole time, John was useless in rescue situations. More useless than he normally felt. He'd been worried Phillip would like Molly better than him. That Phillip would look back over his early years with his father and know with certainty that he'd been slighted. Robbed of a childhood with a capable parent. And now, holy shit. When Phillip realized that apparently some people could achieve flight, he'd wonder even more why John had always been holding him back. John would be a small footnote in the book of Phillip's future.

With his grip on reality slipping, John decided to relinquish all control. He slumped forward and closed his eyes and disengaged from the world for a moment.

It's a big job trying to expand your brain to encompass a broader reality. Sometimes, you just had to rest.

4

The light turned green and Denise hit the gas. The wheels screeched, which was pretty gratifying. She wanted to contribute as much as she could, and now that Beth had flown after them, the best she could offer John was a chance at catching up. John's grip on her hand loosened and she realized he'd passed out.

She'd only met him two days ago, but she already knew that he was so much better than he thought he was. After he was left alone to raise Phillip, he began to focus on everything that had gone wrong in his own childhood and all the things he had messed up as a parent. Somewhere along the way, he'd decided that other parents around him weren't making any mistakes. So each one he made stung even deeper, solidifying his growing belief that he was a failure.

But Denise had never met someone with that much conviction. His devotion to Phillip was staggeringly beautiful. And his ability to pivot and grow as a human was not only admirable, but also sexy as hell. Sure, he had a slouchy handsomeness about him, but his self-awareness catapulted him into something like a movie star. Even though his body had gone limp, she gripped his hand even tighter, her other hand clutching the steering wheel as she barreled toward his son.

She felt John there next to her, the two of them moving at the same speed. If she disregarded the street and the planet and the sun and the entire universe rotating around, the two of them were perfectly still. Perfectly in sync.

"Beth looked fucking beautiful," Taylor said, startling Denise because she'd forgotten he was there.

About a minute after Beth had flown away, Denise had lost sight of her. Watching her sister shoot into the air was one of the most graceful things she'd ever seen. She knew Beth could fly. But never with purpose like that. Flying could be her whole life. There was so much she could accomplish.

"She should never, ever stop flying again," Denise said.

Taylor's phone buzzed. He answered and after listening for a moment he said, "Beth found them. At a diner."

John woke as they pulled into the parking lot. Denise spotted the car they'd been following parked near the door. John blinked. Then blinked again.

"Ask me anything," Denise said to John.

"Can you fly too?"

"No," she said. She figured she'd save her big reveal for later.

Taylor graciously tapped John's shoulder and Denise watched the color come back to his face. A wave of relief washed over him. "You're doing that, aren't you?" John said.

Taylor shrugged. "I have no idea what you mean." He let go of John and got out of the car.

Denise turned to John. "You trust me?"

"I strangely do," John said.

"Taylor and I are going to get Phillip and bring him back here."

"I'd appreciate that very much."

"Can I sleep over again later?"

"Yes."

Denise looked into his eyes and he looked back at her, and she desperately wanted to be a part of whatever came next for him.

He nodded as if he understood. So she nodded back.

Then Beth slid into the backseat. "Are you planning to wait here until they leave so we can chase them again? Can't say I'd mind. But just wanted us all to be on the same page."

John broke their gaze and turned toward Beth. "How do you do it?" he asked.

"Flying? I have no idea," Beth said.

As Denise got out of the car, John leaned forward again, sucking air as if the explanation were mixed in with its molecules.

Taylor laughed from where he leaned against the truck parked next to them.

"Come on," Denise said. "Give him a break. It's a lot to take in."

"I'm not laughing at him," Taylor said. "I'm laughing at you."

The blood rushed to her face and caused the bruises across her cheeks to pulse with pain.

"But I know you want to help either way. It's not just because you're in love with him."

"We should have let that woman kick you a few more times."

He fell in step behind her as she walked as fast as she could toward the front door of the diner.

5

Phillip knew that he'd blown it. Now that they'd left the motel, how would his dad possibly find him? His mom sat across from him in the booth, some sunlight from the window splashing across her hands. After doing his best to stall, he was going to have to eat something even though he'd never been less hungry in his life.

"What's your favorite diner food? she said.

"Pancakes," Phillip said.

"Yeah, me too." She sighed and pushed the menu away from her. "We aren't going to get to know each other this way."

"What do you mean?" Phillip said.

She rubbed her hands together and the sunlight ducked in between her fingers. "I'll tell you something important."

He nodded.

"You know that Sammy guy I was talking about? Right before I came here, he asked me to marry him."

Phillip felt a rush of elation. First it was Mrs. Clark and now it was his mom speaking to him like an adult. "Do you love him?" he asked, because it seemed like the right thing. He couldn't read her face.

"No," she said. She looked disappointed herself. "But I think I could. I just haven't let myself love anyone. Not since your dad."

"You loved Dad?"

"I sure did. Like a whole shitload."

"What happened to the shitload?" Phillip said with his teeth partially gritted. But he had to get that word out. It was important to the conversation.

"Who knows what happens to shitloads," she said. "One of the mysteries of life."

Phillip swallowed even though his mouth was dry. "There's a girl I like," he said.

"Really?" his mom said, completely invested in what he might say next. As if Phillip was the most interesting person in the world. "What's the shitload factor?"

"Pretty high," Phillip said. "But she told me she was holding hands with another boy."

"That's probably because she doesn't know how awesome it would be to hold hands with you."

"Thanks, Mom. Yeah, I bet I'd be really good at it."

"I must meet this girl. Maybe when we get back."

Phillip took a big breath. "Do we really have to go on the road trip?"

Doubt and concern flashed across her face. "Do you not want to?"

"I do," Phillip stammered. "But I don't know, maybe..."

Phillip looked across the diner and there was the naked woman. Even though she was clothed every other time he'd seen her, he couldn't help thinking of her as "the naked woman."

Everything was about to happen. Everything was about to change. His mom would know he'd called them. She would feel betrayed. She might never talk to him again. Forever this time. If only the naked woman wasn't here. If only he and his mom could finish this conversation.

6

Oh shit. Molly was something else. Taylor watched Denise stutter step when she got a good glimpse of her too. It was shocking. He could write a full album about that face. For a full thirty seconds, Taylor forgot to check if she had the kid with her.

Then he saw the kid notice Denise and he looked spooked. In fact, it looked like he was signaling for her to stop.

Taylor cut across the diner and stepped in front of Denise. "Hold up a second," he said.

"What?"

Her adrenaline was so high her whole body was nearly throbbing with her heartbeat.

"Just a feeling I got," Taylor said. "Call it my spider sense."

7

Beth couldn't sit in the car any longer. After the dazzling chase from the sky and her exultant call to Taylor revealing the boy's location, it really sucked to be sidelined with John like they were extras filming a movie, waiting to walk by in the background after the director called action.

John was craned forward, peering at the diner as if he could see through walls. Given what she and her siblings could do, maybe he could.

"Can you see through walls?" she asked.

"No," he said. He sounded moderately disappointed in himself.

He appeared to be unable to look her in the eye now. Definitely possible he was craning forward in his seat to put some distance between them.

"Are you scared of me?" she asked.

"A little. I'm a little scared of all of you."

"You know what I'm scared of?" Beth said.

John finally turned to look at her. "I wouldn't know. Hope it's not heights."

"Bees. I'm deathly afraid of bees."

"Because their stingers hurt? You know they die after they sting you?"

"Yes, I knew that. But one of them killed my dad." Strange how she'd now told two people in the last couple of days about this and she'd never told Fran. "You know what else?"

Beth knew that John was hanging onto her words now. His constitution had nearly fully returned since he'd passed out.

"My dad had a power too. He had super strength. He once picked up our car with one hand so he could get a ball I'd kicked under it. Another time, he punched a hole through a brick wall when our neighbors' house caught on fire and their cats were able to escape through it. I miss him so much. When he died, our family fell apart. And that's why you see us how we are now. This is the version of us without him."

"Are there other people like you?" John said. "With powers?"

"I have no idea," Beth said. "But there was absolutely no one like him. No one."

John turned around to look at the diner again, but he'd stopped straining forward in his seat. "I'm sorry about that."

"Thanks," Beth said. "I never get to talk about Dad like that. I appreciate it. Felt good."

"I know what you mean. There's really no one I was ever able to talk to about Molly and Phillip."

Beth squeezed her eyes closed. She thought of the times over the last couple days that she'd talked to Denise about her dreams. "Denise is a really great listener. I'm glad you have her."

"You think I have her?"

"Absolutely."

"That's good. Because I need her."

Beth thought of how much she needed Denise now. Even Taylor. And the thought of no longer having her mom caused crippling devastation.

"I can't sit in this car anymore," she said. "We have to get out of here."

8

"We have to do this trip, Phillip," his mom said. "It's really important."

Phillip thought if he had a few minutes that his mom would agree to take him home and end this kidnapping. But she seemed a little aggravated now. Like he was letting her down.

"You said you wanted to go, right?" she said. "Don't overthink it. This is something we can do together. And then we'll come back. As soon as we're done."

"But what if we get in trouble?"

"What do you mean? I'm your mom. We won't get in trouble. Moms go on vacation with their children all the time."

This wasn't how he thought this conversation would go at all. "What about Dad though?"

"I called him, Phillip. I let him know we were safe."

"You called him?"

"Of course. We can't just run off without calling him."

"Isn't he worried? Didn't he want to talk to me? Maybe I should call him too before we leave."

"What would he be worried about? I'm your mom. We're fine. Totally fine. You don't need to call him. Not yet. Let's start our trip first."

"I just want him to know I'm okay. That we thought of the plan together."

"What are you saying? That you're being kidnapped. That I'm taking you against your will? I thought we had something going here."

"We do, Mom. We really do. But do we have to leave right now?"

Phillip looked over to the man who had stopped the naked woman from approaching them. He tried to signal him that maybe they should come over after all.

9

Denise thought of John waiting in the car. By now, he probably imagined they'd started some sort of plan, that they'd at least confronted Molly. But instead, she and Taylor were standing next to a table populated by two elderly couples who kept glaring at them and whispering loudly to each other.

"Just eat your food," Denise said to one of the elderly women. "It's going to get cold."

"It's a bowl of fruit," the elderly woman said.

"It'll go rotten then."

Taylor put himself between the table and Denise.

"I'm going to need you to stop doing that," Denise said.

"Keep your cool," he said.

"I'm cool."

And then things escalated.

10

It was falling apart for Molly. She had made strides toward a reconciliation. Toward a place in Phillip's life. But she'd been pushing the Mom thing. The moniker and the authority she assumed it granted her. Even as the words were leaving her mouth, she knew they were wrong. She could hear it. I'm your mom. I'm in charge. Do what I say. She saw the doubt seeping into his eyes. The tiniest glint of fear. She was ruining everything, but she couldn't stop. She needed this trip. It was the only way forward. The only possible future for them. Didn't Phillip see that? There was nothing else for her now. He needed to see it. He needed to understand.

He needed to come with her.

11

His mom stood up. Angry and scared and fiercely determined. Phillip couldn't talk himself out of this situation. He wasn't sure why he ever thought he could.

She leaned toward him, her hands gripping the edge of the table. "You're coming with me. You'll thank me later."

"But I want to go home first," Phillip said. "To pack some things. Why do we have to sneak away?"

Another flash of anger. "We're not sneaking away, Phillip. How many times do I have to tell you?"

In that moment, he felt so badly for her. He'd let her believe the road trip was a possibility and now she felt she had to fight for it. He'd given her hope, probably for the first time in a long time. But seeing her at her lowest moment, he truly understood her. She felt more like his mom than at any other time since they'd been reunited yesterday. His whole family dynamic made sense.

His dad was lonely. His mom was alone.

"Phillip!" the naked woman said in an overly loud voice. "I can't believe I ran into you here."

His mom looked so confused that Phillip almost started explaining every-thing to her.

"You know this lady?" she said.

Before Phillip could respond, the naked woman pushed her way into the booth next to him and put her arm around him. "Get ready," she whispered.

Then his mom screamed. And screamed and screamed and screamed.

12

Molly's anguish was all-encompassing. Taylor watched as she tried to stand and then slumped back into the booth. But the scream never stopped. The elderly couples next to him dropped their silverware and cups in a panicked cacophony.

Taylor was in a brief moment of paralysis. He had never been confronted with such naked emotion. The rest of the world seemed to have stopped existing for Molly. It was only her and her pure horror and sadness. As soon as Denise and Phillip disappeared from view, Molly lost a possible future with Phillip.

Taylor was the only witness to her true devastation. She wasn't a villain. He could see that. He could help her. He knew he could. He'd been exactly where she'd been before. But no one was going to kick her in the ribs. Taylor would protect her.

He didn't even take off his gloves. He just moved toward the table and knelt next to her.

"It's okay," he said.

"My son," she sobbed loudly.

"He's still here. I can take you to him. I can take you right now. You just need to stop screaming."

"How?" she gulped.

A coterie of waitresses and employees along with a man in a suit and a couple of extraneous diners approached them.

"What is going on here?" the man in the suit said.

"Back off," Taylor said. "She just needs a minute. Right, Molly? Let it all out for one minute. Everything inside. And then we go meet up with Phillip."

Molly let it out.

13

Denise watched in horror as Molly had a complete and utter breakdown. She clutched Phillip to her body, and he shook in inconsistent spasms. It must be hard to watch his mother that way. So close to them. Her eyes spinning, the whites eclipsing the pupil. Her chin hinged down to her neck, her tongue poised like a snake. Spittle collected on her lips. Her unnaturally white teeth slick with the residue of fear. They were witnessing true terror.

Why had it taken Taylor so long to approach? And why now, as she tried to quietly slip away with Phillip, past the gathering group of patrons and employees, did Taylor still have his gloves on?

14

Phillip took stock of his body. His arms and his legs and his head were all in the right place. His heart still beat and he felt the blood pulsing out into his body. His nerves jangled and all five of his senses were intact. Everything felt the exact same. Being invisible hadn't changed anything about him.

"No one can see us," he said. Not a question. Just an observation. He liked the way the naked woman was gripping him. Two hands on his upper arms. Guiding him through the diner so they didn't bump into anyone. He felt safe.

"Not a single person in the entire world can see us."

It was as if he and the naked woman were in another realm. An alternate reality placed lightly over his normal reality. Suz might be holding hands with boys, but he was turning invisible and going on adventures.

As they reached the door, the screaming stopped. The man who had arrived with the naked woman was helping his mom sit down in the booth.

"Will she be okay?" Phillip said.

"Yes. Maybe not the same as before. But definitely okay."

"Will she get in trouble?"

"Do you want her to be in trouble?"

"No. I want to go on a road trip with her one day."

His mom continued to wail in the booth, taking huge, deep breaths. The man looked at the crowd still gathered around them and yelled, "Someone bring her a coffee."

"She doesn't like coffee," Phillip said.

The naked woman laughed.

15

When the screaming started, John tried to run into the diner, but Beth grabbed him by the arm. Her feet lifted off the ground and she pulled him up and away from the door. John had barely been an inch off the ground, but it was enough to awe him into submission.

"You'll just throw it off," Beth said.

She was right. He had no business in there.

Then the door of the diner opened on its own. It wobbled slightly and then closed. With no warning sound or rippling of air or flash of light, Denise and Phillip materialized directly in front of him. One second John was bereft, the next second he was reunited with his son.

He throbbed from lack of sleep. He was emotionally drained. He had to pee really badly. So John decided not to think about invisibility right now. It required too much of him to process anything new. He just wanted to be home with Phillip. To feel the normal things settle back into place.

"Come here, man," he said, and Phillip lunged into his arms.

"I'm sorry I don't know your phone number," Phillip said.

"I don't care about that. I don't care about that at all."

16

It bothered Beth that the rescue felt so anticlimactic to her. A man was reunited with his son and here she was wishing she'd been able to fly more. Like her role in everything had been too easy. Like it wasn't fair.

She turned from their loving reunion and looked through the front window of the diner. There was Taylor sitting with Molly at a booth. He was abstractedly reaching under his shirt and pulling at the wrap around his ribs. He looked wan and sweaty and probably needed to go back to the doctor after their adventures today. But he seemed completely focused on Molly. On talking to her. His hands were nowhere near her. Beth understood what he was doing. He was trying to heal without his power. Now that required strength.

In the meantime, Denise had inserted herself into John and Phillip's reunion and in all their hurried talking, Beth kept hearing Phillip refer to Denise as the naked woman and that was absolutely a story she'd love to hear.

Beth thought about joining Taylor and Molly inside, but they were deep into conversation now. Outside, Denise had wrapped her arms around John and Phillip.

She looked around the parking lot. At Molly's car. At John's car. All these earthbound people were going to need to creep slowly home on four tires.

They wouldn't even notice she was gone.

CHAPTER SIXTEEN

KEEPING THE END IN SIGHT

1

Taylor drove Molly's rental car at a nice slow pace. Partly to minimize bumps and the resulting shooting rib pain, but also to maximize the time he had with her. She was way out of his league, but perhaps he could still come out of this experience with a chance.

She sat curled in the passenger seat and had been quiet since their time in the diner booth. He'd somehow, at least for now, convinced her that Phillip hadn't disappeared. That she was having some kind of trauma response. He'd managed to talk her down without the use of his power, and now he found himself piloting her car with no idea what to say.

"Can you take me to see Phillip?" It had been an hour since she'd last spoken.

Everyone had told Taylor it was a bad idea for Molly to go to John's house. Even Beth had pulled him aside to say not to go there. But what did any of them know?

"Hell, yeah," he said. "Great idea."

She shifted in the seat and tucked her legs underneath her.

"So you're an actress, huh?"

"Is anyone what they actually claim to be? I like to act. But if I can't point you to anywhere my work exists, do I get to claim the title?"

"Of course, you do," Taylor said. "You're the one telling your story. If you love acting and you're putting yourself out there and everyone is too stupid to cast you, then you're still an actress."

She smiled in the dwindling light. "Thanks, I appreciate that."

"I tell everyone I'm a musician."

"I've known a lot of musicians," she said, and not in the way he wanted her to say it.

"I play the bass and sing. Write songs. Lead a band. All the stuff that makes other people really cool."

"The ones who think they're cool rarely are."

"I'm too focused on the work aspect. I want to make music for a living. I want it to be my job."

"Yes, exactly," Molly said and untucked her legs from under her. She shifted her body to face him, and it felt like he'd won an initial battle. "And you see other people doing it and wonder, why can't that be me?"

"All the time," Taylor said. "And I'm fucking good."

"Me too."

More than anything, he hoped that Gill had made good on his promise. That his demo would be there at the hospital, and he could play his music for Molly.

"You're never going to make it here," she said. "This is a dead scene."

"It does seem dead," Taylor said, his heart thumping at 120 beats per minute.

"You should come to LA," she said. "That's where you should be."

2

Phillip watched the way his dad and the naked woman pulled toward each other as she drove. Every small jostle of the car moved them closer. Nobody spoke as the sun set on the day. Phillip was exhausted. He couldn't wait to get home to his bed. He wondered where his mom was now. He wondered if he'd ever see her again.

"Mom said I was a shitload," he said.

His dad spun around, a quizzical look on his face. "So she's Mom now?"

"Yes," Phillip said. He looked out the window and recognized the sandwich shop not far from their house. He was almost home.

"I need to tell you something," his dad said. "As your dad."

"I can handle it," Phillip said.

"I no longer have a job."

Phillip tried to remember exactly what his dad did for his job but all that came to mind was that he tucked in his shirts. "It's okay."

"Might get rough for a second."

"I think we can handle it," Phillip said.

"Me too. Thinking about switching it up a little."

"So you won't have to tuck in your shirt anymore?"

His dad laughed. "Maybe not."

The naked woman cleared her throat. "I hate to jump in. But I'm confused. A shitload of what? What did your mom mean?"

"Love, I think," Phillip said.

"A shitload of love?" the naked woman said.

It sounded weird when he heard it that way. "Maybe it was happiness."

"Still not a phrase I'm familiar with," the naked woman said.

His dad pointed out the windshield. "I think you'll get a chance to ask her," he said.

Phillip watched his small house grow near. The car where he'd spent the last 24 hours with his mom sat on the curb out front. His heart leapt at the sight. It was now clear how much he wanted to see her again. As many times as possible.

The naked woman pulled into the driveway, the streetlight flashing across her bruised face. Phillip felt something for her in that moment. How much she'd done for him even though she barely knew him. He leaned forward and whispered in her ear. "Thank you."

She smiled and winced slightly from the pain. Then she got quickly out of the car and moved toward the house.

"Want me to come with you?" his dad said.

"No. I'll be okay," Phillip said.

"Let's not start this whole thing all over."

"No way."

His dad closed his eyes. "I love you," he said. He always closed his eyes when he made a proclamation of love, as if the words required an influx of energy.

Phillip kept his eyes on him. "I love you, too."

His dad nodded before opening his eyes and getting out of the car.

Phillip took a deep breath and opened his door. He could feel his dad watching him from the darkness of the porch.

Then his mom got out of the rental car. "I scared everyone away, huh?"

"Maybe a little," Phillip said.

The man from earlier sat in the driver seat. "Just act like I'm not here," he said.

"Thanks for driving my mom," Phillip said.

"I'm stoked to do it. For real." The man smiled and he looked so much like the naked woman in that moment.

His mom put her hand on his shoulder and moved him away from the car. "I just wanted to say goodbye. I decided to head back to LA tonight. I've wreaked enough havoc."

"You going to marry that Sammy guy?" Phillip said.

"I don't know yet. Probably."

Phillip moved to the end of the driveway, closer to his mom. He attempted to send a psychic message to her that he wanted a hug. "Can we talk every once in a while?"

"Your dad going to be okay with that?"

"He's a shitload, but he's still my dad. It'll be okay."

"Yeah."

But she still hadn't gotten his psychic message yet about the hug. She shuffled her feet, unable to find a place to stand still.

"You're a shitload, too," Phillip said.

"That's true," she said. "We're all shitloads."

Phillip took another step closer. "Can I hug you?"

She didn't even say anything. She just moved toward him and put her arms around him. He rested his head against her chest and felt her heart beating in no discernible pattern.

"You aren't mad at me?" she said. "For what I put you through?"

"We ate at my favorite restaurant and stayed at a hotel. The only problem was we forgot to tell Dad. So next time, we'll tell him first. Before we leave."

"Next time," she said and squeezed him tighter before letting go.

They stared at each other for a moment and then his mom did this half smile, half frown thing.

"I'm leaving before I lose it," she said and got in the car. She waved as the man backed the car out of the driveway.

And that's when he noticed the mailbox open across the street. Suz must be worried about him too.

"Dad?" he called into the darkness.

"Yes?"

"I'm going to check in on Suz."

"Good idea. Tell her if she ever needs to stay here, to get away, she's always welcome. We'll give her a key. And keep some blankets and a pillow near the couch."

"Thanks, Dad," Phillip said. He heard the front door open and the shuffle of bodies. He waited until the front room light snapped on before crossing the street and heading into Suz's backyard.

He had so much to tell her.

3

Like the night she'd left Fran, Beth flew as if she had no idea where she was going. She went higher and higher until she was gasping for air. Then she dove and spun and twisted, the wind whipping against her body until the need was gone. She was meant to fly. She'd always been meant to fly.

She wasn't sure how much time had passed before she pointed herself toward the hospital. She flew closer to the streets until she was able to reacquaint herself with her position on earth, zipping along at a pace faster than she'd ever attempted to fly before.

Then a bug exploded on her forehead and she slowed a bit. But only a bit.

Beth saw the lights of the hospital off in the distance and she got nervous. This was the second act plot twist leading into the third act. This was the part in the movie where she left. She thought about going as high as she could again. She thought about starting somewhere new. But she didn't want to run away anymore. She was going to see this through.

From the sky, she found a dark spot at the top of the parking garage where a light had burnt out, and that's exactly where she landed. Out of breath and covered in sweat. But exhilarated.

She took out her phone and called Taylor.

"There you are," he said. "I wondered if I'd hear from you. I just got to the hospital but I'm in the lobby. I'm too scared to go up."

The relief she felt was immeasurable. "I'm so glad you're here," Beth said. "I'm on the roof."

"Let's go in together."

"Be right there." She hung up and stomped away with her leaden feet in search of an extremely slow-moving elevator.

Beth and Taylor walked into their mom's hospital room to find the bed empty. No sign of the machines that had previously been there. A fresh blanket stretched across the mattress.

The nurse from earlier walked up behind them.

"She's gone," the nurse said, and the words slashed through Beth's skin and burrowed deeper and deeper until they were etched on every bone in her body.

Her legs gave out and Taylor steadied her. She felt an immediate sense of well-being. An urge to say that their mom was in a better place. But she didn't want Taylor to help her through this moment. Beth wanted to feel every single emotion.

She pushed Taylor away and the sadness overwhelmed her again.

"How long has she been gone?" Beth said.

The nurse suddenly clutched at her chest, the color draining from her face. "Oh, I'm so terribly sorry. She's not dead. God, I really said that in a terrible way. She's just moved on. No. God. Not that either. There are too many euphemisms. Someone picked her up. She went home. Like her actual home in this realm of existence." The nurse took a deep breath. "She's alive."

Beth couldn't help it. She lurched forward and hugged the nurse as hard as she could.

"You are such a dear sweet thing," Beth said, her face pressed into the nurse's shoulder.

"You aren't angry?" the nurse said.

Beth hugged her tighter. "Never."

Taylor stepped awkwardly around them, his hands hovering in front of him.

The embrace ended. Beth and the nurse looked at each other for a moment before she sniffed and went back to work.

"That was fucked up," Taylor said.

But Beth was grounded again. Her body had returned to the impermanence of now. This precise moment where her mom was still alive. With no way of knowing if that would be the case with each unfolding moment.

She had to get home.

4

Edna loved her house when it was dark. The shadows were deep fissures across the room, obscuring the emptiness that seemed spotlighted during the day. At night, Edna could believe that Nolan was still there. That maybe his shoes were placed neatly inside the shadow by the back door. That his favorite mug sat on the table, engulfed in darkness next to his favorite chair. That Nolan himself was sprawled on the couch. In moments like this, Edna never wanted the light to come back.

She moved through the front room and toward the stairs. She waited at the bottom, hoping to hear a creak or catch a whiff of Nolan's cologne. He had been the strongest man she'd ever known. Figuratively and literally. Just like their children, he'd possessed a gift. He had supported Edna through their marriage with a steady hand and a calming presence. But he could also uproot a tree from the ground, roots and all. He could crush the front end of a semi-truck with his bare hands. He could break every bone in an arm. He could keep the whole family safe.

Then he was taken out by one of the smallest of God's creatures. A tiny little bee that would die not long after leaving its stinger in Nolan. They left the world together. And that was when Edna had stopped believing. Not just veering away from God. But divesting from any security she'd felt. Stopping any search for meaning. She'd let herself down by not staying stronger. She'd let her children down. Now, at the end of her life, she could show her children how to die gracefully. How to be strong in the face of oblivion.

Her illness had brought her family back together. Now it was up to Edna to make sure they stayed together. In a life largely devoid of meaning, their bond was the light that cast away the shadows. But in their version, it revealed all the little intricacies of their shared life. Their shared path. Edna planned to stay alive as long as she could until her children understood the power they possessed. Not just their collective gifts, but the power of their family.

Strength was not running away.

Edna laughed at how earnest and serious her thoughts had become. Maybe the tumor had eaten away at her fear.

She heard a car in the driveway. Of all of them, Beth would understand why she'd had Hank take her home. Why she wanted to end her days here in the house. She stepped to the dining table that Nolan had carved from a fallen tree and waited for her children to join her.

It felt nice to wait when she had so little time left.

5

Denise nestled into John's bed while he changed. Her head sunk into the pillow, and she clutched his blankets to her chest. She wanted to slip her head underneath to finish the cocoon. She'd emerge in the morning as a brand-new person.

"Don't you want to spend time with Phillip tonight?" she said, groggy from the day.

"I just wanted him home," John said as he pulled a t-shirt over his skinny frame. "I don't want to smother him."

"Is the girl across the street his girlfriend?"

John slid into the bed and pulled her toward him as if he'd been doing it his whole life. Like he'd been in this bed practicing since the day Molly left.

"I don't think so," he said. "Not yet. Maybe one day. She's got a rough home life and right now, she needs a friend."

"Does he go over there a lot?"

"I'm starting to think he probably does." John laughed. "We have some secrets I guess."

"But that's okay," Denise said.

"Yes. I think it is."

Denise closed her eyes and felt his warm breath on her shoulder. She'd spent so many years trying to fill up everyone around her, it was nice to feel her empty spaces solidifying. She'd wanted to find Phillip for John. But also for herself. She felt satiated and full and happy and solid. Their bodies fit perfectly together. She was aware of the space she occupied. Her weight. Her meaning.

"Can we talk about..." He trailed off.

"Not tonight," Denise said. She didn't want to get into her dad and her siblings and their unexplainable powers. Now was not the time to explain herself.

His breathing steadied until she was sure that he'd fallen asleep. Tomorrow Denise would need to return to her family. They would have to figure out how best to care for their mom and what they would do when she was gone. They would also need to make some sense of today and everything they'd accomplished. Maybe they didn't have to hide anymore. Maybe they'd find others like them out there.

But tonight, she wanted to feel full. She wanted to feel needed. She wanted to need.

"Are you awake?" John asked, his voice barely a whisper.

"I'm awake."

"Will you do it?" he said.

"Do what?" she asked, but she knew exactly what he was asking.

"The thing you did in the diner."

Denise took a deep breath, flexed that special muscle, and disappeared.

"Did you do it?" he asked.

"Yes."

The room was so dark, and Denise was buried under the blankets, John had no way of knowing.

He squeezed her tighter. "I can still feel you," he said in hushed awe. "I can still feel you."

"I can still feel you too," Denise said.

There was no way to know if John was invisible too.

Later

THE EXCITING CONCLUSION

CHAPTER SEVENTEEN

REHEARSING THE END

1

Mr. Scully waited on the stairs as Renata turned toward the camera. Beth crouched down and zoomed in, hoping to fill the screen with Renata's sweaty glowing face.

"Keeping the end in sight is the key to a great workout," Renata said. Flatter than the last take. They could both feel Mr. Scully watching silently. Renata couldn't perform with anyone watching.

She lifted a Pop Tart, which had been Beth's idea, and took a big bite. "The one bite reward."

Beth pulled back to make in room in the frame for one of Renata's cartoon monsters that she would add later.

"Hey!" Renata said to something that no one could see yet. "Give that back!"

She pretended to struggle with the monster, but then looked directly into the camera. "This isn't a good take."

"Agreed," Beth said. "Let's cut."

"The magic word," Mr. Scully said as he descended the remaining few stairs. "And let me get out of here. I know I messed that one up for you."

"No, you didn't, Mr. Scully," Renata said.

Beth turned toward him and smiled. "Of course, you did, Mr. Scully. But we're still happy to see you."

"Your mom's asleep," he said and patted Beth on the back. "See you next week."

The moment the front door shut behind him, Renata and Beth began laughing maniacally.

"I just can't," Renata said.

"I wish you never said anything," Beth said.

"I'm not the one who said it," Renata said.

Beth watched her laughing, her face flushed. She loved her so much in that moment. Not like before. This was a deep love. Like family. And it was good to have. Denise didn't come by nearly as much now that she'd moved in with John. And Taylor was still in LA playing shows with his new band and trying to convince Molly not to marry that Sammy guy.

"I merely wondered," Beth said, "if he takes his pants fully off or just pops it out through the zipper."

"Your mom is not having sex up there."

"You don't know that." Beth smiled. "I better go check on her though. Let's nail that scene when I get back."

"Yes, boss," Renata said.

Beth stomped up the stairs to her mom's room. She looked into her own room on the way. She'd left it exactly the same since she'd moved in permanently. She liked living in a little time capsule. On the nights that Denise came over, she still curled up in bed with Beth and they talked the whole night. So much better without a phone between them. The food dreams had completely stopped.

Beth knocked lightly on her mom's door. "Mom?"

No answer.

She entered the room and immediately knew everything was going to be different. Beth didn't even look at her mom. She couldn't yet. Instead, she stared at a picture of her Mom and Dad on the dresser. They looked so happy. Invulnerable. Perfect.

Then something tapped on the window. A hypnotic buzz in between taps. Listening to it made Beth's head wobble. She knew exactly what was behind that curtain.

She took a deep breath and walked around the bed to the window. She pulled the curtain and there it was. A small bee, perfectly striped in black and

Sun splashed across the floor, flickering through clouds and tree branches. Yet still bright enough to completely engulf the bee.

Tap. Tap. Tap.

Beth closed her eyes and leaned forward, the buzzing getting closer and closer. But she knew what she had to do. Her fingers groped along the top of the window until she found the latch. She unlocked it and then grabbed the base of the window and pulled it up.

She stepped back and watched the bee work its way toward freedom. Except that it wasn't freedom. Not yet.

Beth leaned forward again, the bee only inches from her face. She put both of her palms on the screen and pushed until it popped from its frame and toppled to the ground.

The bee buzzed louder but Beth didn't move. It grazed her cheek as it passed, the flutter of its wings like a whisper.

Then it exploded from the house and took to the air. For a moment, Beth felt the urge to follow it. To fly away from everything about to happen in this house. To see where it might take her. Instead, she watched the sun surround the bee until it completely disappeared.

As if it had never been there at all.

ABOUT THE AUTHOR

Josh Denslow is the author of the collection *Not Everyone is Special*. He currently lives in Barcelona with his three boys, his amazing wife, his mother-in-law, four cats, a dog, hundreds of books, and an electronic drum kit.

ACKNOWLEDGMENTS

Super Normal (previously known as *All that Remains*, and even more previously known as *Touch*) has been with me for nearly two decades. I remember talking into a voice recorder (yes, a voice recorder!) on a long drive from Los Angeles to Chicago, recording what would become the first ideas for this book. None of those ideas survived.

I rewrote *Super Normal* four times from scratch over the years, in addition to all the tinkering between do-overs, and for every iteration I have to thank a different group of people. And I think that's the best way to handle this acknowledgments section; one iteration at a time.

In the early days, especially before there was a full draft, I thank T. Duncan Anderson for reading pages, offering thoughts, and always believing that I could write a full novel. And even though it's maybe not customary to thank an agent who gave you a pass, I must thank Meredith Kaffel Simonoff for being the first agent to ever reach out to me from a story I had published in a journal. Because of our correspondence, I pushed myself to complete a first draft. It wasn't very good. Thanks for reading anyway, Meredith.

All of my drafts were read with care and a critical eye by Pam Susemiehl, and I'm grateful to have her as a friend and a reader. Many of my ideas would have died on the page without her nudges. Pam helped me with the next two versions during the dark years when it seemed I would never get it right. During this time, I also want to thank two of my favorite people in the world, Tim and Michelle Burke, who read a draft and made me feel like a really cool guy for writing a book.

Intense gratitude to Key K Bird, one of my earliest writer friends and publishers who helped me get to the draft that was ultimately accepted by Stillhouse. They spent an exhilarating number of weeks with me reading each chapter as I was churning them out and then discussing with me. It was such an amazing learning experience to work with them like that, and I will never forget it. I think they will be surprised though to see how the novel transitioned into what is now called *Super Normal*. It's a completely different book than what Key and I did (no more evil kidnapper with the creepy basement!), but without them, I wouldn't have found a home at Stillhouse Press.

One more big thank you before I launch into the final leg of this epically long acknowledgments page goes to Eric Newman. He read the draft that Stillhouse ultimately accepted and gave me some truly profound insight into my failings as a writer that I don't think many people would have the courage to tell someone. Things I needed to hear. Things we all need to be talking about. Thank you Eric for being a true friend and gracious reader.

Oh Stillhouse. The most patient and understanding and wonderful group of people you will ever meet. If there is a pandemic raging and everyone is in lockdown and you start doubting yourself and you turn down an offer of publication because you want to write your novel one more time from scratch because you feel very strongly that you are finally ready, then I suggest you get Stillhouse Press on your side. Thank you for waiting while I wrote a completely new novel than the one you previously accepted, and for reading it and accepting it again, and for always believing in me. Thank you, Scott W. Berg for getting on the phone with me for hours and just talking about this book, but also about life and how hard it is to know what we're really doing. Thanks to Rebecca Burke for that exciting acceptance call, and to Linda Hall for guiding me through the process with a smile. But the biggest thanks of all to Carol Mitchell, my editor at Stillhouse, who understood exactly what I was doing, and who I always felt wanted me to succeed as much as I did. Adding another ten thousand words was the perfect note (no matter how much I grumbled), and the characters are stronger because of her discerning eye. I wish Carol could read all my books forever.

During this strange twenty years, I wasn't only working on *Super Normal*! What gave you that idea? Leland Cheuk swooped in to change my life and give me a new boost of confidence in my own work when he published my story collection *Not Everyone is Special* at 7.13 Books. There were many times when I felt like giving up, and I truly believe I wouldn't be here with a second book without Leland. I also finished three drafts of a very long, sort of epic novel that I hope one day finds a home too. But writing it changed everything for me. I discovered myself in that novel and it's the reason that I knew I was finally ready to get *Super Normal* into its final state. So the people who helped me work on other projects were actually helping me with this novel as well, however indirectly, and I want to thank a few of them here. First is KC Mead-Brewer who I have learned so much from reading her stories, but also her indispensable notes. Also to Mark Jednaszewski who not only read many of my other projects and offered the most insightful notes, he also kept me on task with my rewrites for *Super Normal* as I alternately plowed ahead and faltered. And to the many editors who published my work during the last twenty years and the many friends who offered advice and guidance. That means it's time for my shoutout to Tod Goldberg who I will always think of as a mentor and a friend.

Thank you to my team at Bookshop.org for believing in me and getting excited at the right times. Special thanks to Steph Opitz and Angela Januzzi who were always available for side chats about the crazy world of writing, and to Rob Bieselin for all the artwork advice and advertising assistance. And thank you so very much to my early readers who provided the blurbs that brought me to tears every time: Kevin Wilson, Matthew Salesses, Kimberly King Parsons, Megan Giddings, and Kalani Pickhart.

Twenty years is a long time for a project to live inside of a person, and there is no way that I haven't forgotten someone. Trust me when I say that I am thanking you right here. Your help lives on in all my work, and I know I'm surely going to be kicking myself as time goes on. I will make it up to you!

Now we're ready to get personal! To my mother-in-law: Thank you for making room for me in your family and always pushing me to be better. To my children, Elijah, Ezra, and Moses: I love you so much. Your joy for life and abundant curiosity makes me want to laugh harder, cry more, write louder, and take bigger chances. I'm so lucky that I get to experience every day with you, and I hope to make you proud.

And now, an earnest message to the absolute love of my life. If you aren't the love of my life, no need to read this section at all. You can just go about your day. I'll wait a second. Okay. To Rebecca: I know I say this a lot, but it's always true, none of this would have happened without you. I love the life we have created, and I am truly lucky to start every day knowing that I have your love and support and friendship. Also, get this. I got everyone to leave this page. They're all gone. It's just you and I here at the end of the acknowledgments. So I have a very important question for you, my love. Want to make out?